PRISONER OF THE BLACK HAWK

A. L. TAIT

Kane Miller
A DIVISION OF EDC PUBLISHING

First American Edition 2017
Kane Miller, A Division of EDC Publishing

Copyright © A.L Tait, 2015

First published in Australia and New Zealand in 2015 by Hachette Australia
(an imprint of Hachette Australia Pty Limited), this North American edition
is published by arrangement with Hachette Australia Pty Ltd.

For information contact:
Kane Miller, A Division of EDC Publishing
P.O. Box 470663
Tulsa, OK 74147-0663
www.kanemiller.com
www.edcpub.com
www.usbornebooksandmore.com

Library of Congress Control Number: 2016955643

Printed and bound in the United States of America
5 6 7 8 9 10

ISBN: 978-1-61067-623-6

For Max, Noah, Arabella, Declan, Charlotte, Jake,
Gemma and Elliot

Heads on 'em like mice

Chapter One

Quinn Freeman ducked as a wooden pole whistled past the left side of his head. Hands up to defend his face, he stood with feet apart, breathing heavily, ready for his opponent's next move. He didn't have to wait long, as the heavy stick swung back at him, this time low enough to sweep his feet from under him. Quinn jumped, grabbing hold of the mast next to him, and swung himself up onto a thin beam fixed between it and the smaller mast nearby, running lightly along it to evade his adversary. Reaching the end of the pole, he somersaulted off – just because, he'd recently discovered, he could – and turned back to face his "foe" in triumph.

Zain swung the stick back, and rested it on his shoulder. "Very good, Quinn Freeman," he said, with a half smile.

Quinn stood up a little straighter – this was high praise from his captain.

"Next time, however," Zain continued, this time baring his teeth in a wide smile that gave Quinn the shivers, "perhaps try it without the jester's acrobatics. Overconfidence often leads to embarrassment at best – and a bloody, painful death at worst. Remember, always stay on your feet."

Quinn blushed, and looked around. His friend Ash and the other *Libertas* crew members at the morning training session were all trying to look busy, practicing their own attack and defense moves, but Quinn knew they were smirking at him.

"Ah, Zain," said a quavering voice behind them, "it is nothing but the exuberance of youth."

All eyes turned to Cleric Greenfield, the wizened, gray-haired man acting as the King's representative on board for this voyage. The *Libertas* was one of three ships taking part in a year-long race to map the world, with the winning captain able to claim the prize of his choice. In Zain's case, that prize was freedom. John Dolan, captain of the *Wandering Spirit*, had chosen gold and glory; Odilon of Blenheim and his *Fair Maiden* crew were trying to win a seat on the King's own council – and the power that went with it.

Neither Dolan nor Odilon was happy with Zain's inclusion in the race, feeling that, as a slave, he was not in their league.

From what Quinn had witnessed, this was true – but not in the way that the other explorers thought. Both Odilon and Dolan had proven themselves to be treacherous, untrustworthy characters, and those were two words that Quinn would never use about his captain, who commanded the admiration and respect of everyone on board the *Libertas*.

Ostensibly, Cleric Greenfield was on board to "keep an eye" on Zain, to ensure he didn't sail away and never return. But, given that Zain's wife and daughter were tucked up in the King's castle in Verdania and, given that the old man had little chance of stopping Zain doing *anything*, it was clear to everyone on the *Libertas* that Cleric Greenfield's role was nominal at best. Still, he was treated with respect by everyone on board.

"Of course," said Zain now, with a slight bow. "But exuberance can get a person into a lot of trouble."

The cleric laughed, his whole body shaking in its coarse, brown robe. "What's youth without trouble?" he asked with a wink, taking Quinn by surprise. He'd never really considered the fact that the cleric had once been young, but, of course, he must have been. And, judging by that comment, young and cheeky.

Zain's laugh boomed across the deck in response. "Too true," he said to the cleric.

"Speaking of trouble," Zain continued, turning back to face the assembled crew, "just because we have not yet run into the Gelynions again does not mean the threat has passed. We must remain vigilant. We must remain prepared. We must remain ready."

There was silence while everyone on board considered their last run-in with the fierce men from the neighboring kingdom of Gelyn, who seemed determined to not only map the world first, but to destroy everyone and everything in their path along the way. Quinn shuddered as he remembered his encounter with Morpeth, the huge Deslondic mercenary who acted as "advisor" to Juan Forden, the Gelynion explorer with a formidable reputation. Quinn certainly didn't want to see either of them at close quarters ever again – no matter how vigilant, prepared or ready he might be.

"Right," said Zain. "As you were."

With that, the crew dispersed, muttering amongst themselves. Heading down to his cabin, Quinn noticed that Cook and Dilly went out of their way to stay clear of him, and he sighed.

It was this kind of reaction that had led his family to keep a secret for fourteen years: the secret of Quinn's unusually good memory. Unfortunately for Quinn, the *Libertas* crew had witnessed his freakish memory in action when he'd learned a strange language in a day – to save them all from certain death. But while most of them had managed to accept it – *managed*, Quinn knew, because Zain accepted it and they followed his lead – Cook and

Dilly were different, choosing to avoid Quinn, frightened by what they'd seen.

Which was exactly the reaction Quinn's family had tried to shield him against.

Thinking about it made Quinn long for the safety of his little home. At this time of the morning, his da and brothers would be out in the fields, plowing or fencing or tending the family's small herd of cattle. His mam would be in the cozy kitchen with its stone hearth, cooking up a batch of wheat cakes for morning tea, humming as she worked, sunlight streaming through the windows onto the big wooden table.

At least, he thought that's what they'd be doing.

The truth was, Quinn had no idea what time it was in Markham right now. Just like he had no idea why the stars in the night sky looked different here, why the deep ocean changed color as they sailed south, or, frankly, where in the world they were.

There was so much Quinn didn't know that it made his head hurt. Often. He fingered the animal tooth he'd found months before, and had carried as a good luck talisman ever since.

One thing he'd learned in his four and a half months at sea was that all the worrying and head hurting in the world wouldn't change anything. Not when you were on a boat, sailing into the unknown, trying to map a world that may or may not be round. Or potentially sailing right off the edge, if the world were flat, into the waiting jaws of Genesi, the dragon at the end of the world.

Nope, thinking about that stuff didn't change anything. Which was just one of the reasons that Quinn sometimes wished that his brain didn't remember *everything*.

Opening the door of his little cabin, Quinn's heart sank when he realized that his cabinmate was in residence: Kurt, the Northern boy they'd rescued from a frozen ice village. From the way that Kurt was standing awkwardly in the middle of the cabin, Quinn knew he'd been snooping around Quinn's desk again. Not that he could prove it. Kurt was too quick for that. But Quinn knew just the same – and Kurt's sly smile told Quinn that he knew that Quinn knew.

Quinn wished, as he did most days, that he could wipe that smile off Kurt's face . . . all the while knowing that he did not want to deal with his captain (and the consequences) if he did so.

The way the Northerner carried on, you'd think that Zain, Quinn and the *Libertas* crew had wrenched him from the bosom of a loving family, instead of saving his boots (and the rest of him) from certain death by Gelynion sword. Even if they'd simply driven off the Gelynions, the other boy would have had no chance alone in the ice and snow.

It seemed that the way Kurt saw it, though, they had deprived him of the only home he'd ever known – and if he had to suffer, then so did Quinn. Which was why he was now sitting in the corner, fiddling with the shard of rock that he always had with him, glowering as Quinn tried to go about his work.

The work. Even the thought of it was enough to banish Kurt from Quinn's mind. The work was the one thing about this whole crazy expedition that Quinn really loved. When Master Blau had dragged him off to his mapmaker school, Quinn had been dubious to say the least. He loved books and learning, but he knew that making maps meant actually going out into the world to see what was there.

For starters, Quinn had been firmly in the camp that thought all of these ships were going to sail over the edge of the world. Part of him still was, even though they'd been sailing for months now, with no end in sight to the briny ocean. Just because they hadn't gotten there yet, didn't mean the end wasn't coming . . .

In the meantime, Quinn was doing his utmost to create the best, most detailed map he could, because if Zain won, Quinn would also win a parcel of land for his family. And with six sons to worry about, that land would go a long way towards wiping the worried frown from his da's face forever.

He dipped the small brush he'd made from a twig and feathers into the pale-green ink that Ash had created for him from her ever-growing collection of exotic plants, using it to shade a section of coastline. Ash had stowed away on board the *Libertas* before they'd sailed from Verdania, and, when discovered, had managed to convince Zain to let her stay on board – on the condition that she masquerade as a boy and that no one discover her secret.

"There's no point, you know." Kurt's voice broke into Quinn's thoughts, startling him.

"No point in what?" asked Quinn without looking around, staring at his map. The Verdanians had sailed directly west from their homeland, striking land after many weeks. Zain had decided they would go north from there, and north they'd gone, with Quinn tracking the progress of the coastline as they passed it. The sea on that route had been a thrashing, squalling beast of dark navy blue, topped with whitecaps and lashed by storms.

"This mapping business," continued Kurt. "You're never going to be able to show it to anyone."

Quinn finished putting color on a small cove, then turned to face the other boy. Kurt was sitting, slumped against the wall, under the hammock that had been slung between the walls of Quinn's cabin to accommodate him.

Quinn sighed. "And why is that?" he asked, though he knew full well what Kurt was going to say. The same thing he'd said the other twenty-seven times he'd started this conversation.

"You won't get back home," said the blond boy now, a smile of satisfaction creeping over his face. "We're all going to die out here. You should have left me where I was."

Quinn sighed again. "We've been over this, Kurt," he said, keeping his voice even. If there was one thing he'd learned from dealing with five brothers, it was that it never paid to be the first one to raise your voice. If you got emotional, they knew there was a weak spot, and if there was a weak spot . . .

"If we'd left you where you were, you'd be dead already. Those Gelynions were not there to tuck you into bed."

Kurt blanched. "So you say," he muttered.

Quinn shook his head, annoyed at himself. Bringing up the Gelynions was a low blow – after all, they had killed Kurt's parents, along with many other members of his village. Quinn did feel sorry for the younger boy – but he also remembered Morpeth telling Zain that Kurt had translated documents for the invaders, trying to save his own skin.

Another reason Quinn was happy to keep the Northerner at a wary distance.

"Why don't you just sit back and enjoy the ride?" Quinn said now, trying to forestall further conversation. "It's not like you even have to *do* anything to earn your keep."

So far Zain had seemed happy enough to let Kurt sulk and waft about the *Libertas* like a black mood, which was another mark against him as far as Quinn was concerned. Not that Quinn didn't enjoy what he was doing, and he didn't even mind the stints he took up the ship's tallest mast on watch, because they gave him an even better perspective of the stars, the current, the landfall and all the other tools that he used to make his maps as accurate as possible. He just felt that Kurt had too much time on his hands and he was using that time to annoy Quinn.

"Only because *you* won't let me help," said Kurt, frustrated. "I helped my father with book work."

Quinn exhaled sharply. Surely Kurt wasn't going to go over this territory as well. "It's not *your* job," he responded. "It's *mine*." There was no way he was letting Kurt, with his sly ways, get hold of the map.

Ash had laughed at him when Quinn had raised his concerns with her. "You sound like your da," she'd laughed. "What can he possibly do here? He's surrounded by people, he's getting farther and farther from everything he knows and he doesn't even speak Verdanian. He's probably just trying to find a way to feel part of things."

He can watch, thought Quinn. Like he was doing now. Sitting in the corner, watching everything Quinn did.

This *watching* meant that Quinn had stopped writing notes on his cabin wall, as had been his habit before Kurt moved in, and he was now keeping everything in his head. It was probably being overly cautious but he wasn't taking chances. He'd only been at sea a few months and already he was less trusting. Having all your food stolen and being left for dead by another Verdanian competitor could do that to a person. Quinn's hand tightened around his brush as he thought of Dolan, the famed Verdanian

10

explorer and his mapmaker, Ira, who had been Quinn's nemesis at scribe school, as Master Blau's mapmaking school had been known.

That lack of trust was also why Quinn had taken the step of creating an entirely false drawing, complete with inaccurate calculations, which he worked on openly in his cabin. It was just different enough from his real map that it wouldn't look fake, but anyone who tried to use it would find themselves very quickly off course – or run aground.

He worked on and stored the *real* map in Cleric Greenfield's cozy cabin. Quinn had said nothing of Kurt when he'd explained his idea to the cleric, instead saying he was worried that the map would be stolen – by Gelynions or others – and that he wanted to keep it safe.

Once the cleric had agreed, it had taken only half a day to create the "new" map, and to hide the real one away in the old man's desk. So far, it hadn't proved too difficult to update his real map in secret while ostentatiously making changes to the fake one, like he was doing right now.

The cleric was the only one who knew that there were two maps, and he had promised to keep Quinn's secret, though he had questioned why Zain could not know. The truth was that Quinn didn't want his suspicions about Kurt to be made light of again – Zain tended to think that Quinn was too hard on Kurt and that Kurt just needed time to settle in. But Quinn had told the cleric that the fewer people who knew, the safer the map would be, and he had seemed satisfied with that.

A shout from overhead brought Quinn back to the present. Straining to hear, he waited for the shout again – and soon it came.

"Port!" Jericho was calling, over the sound of the waves and the seabirds. "Port to port!"

A port, out here on the edge of the world?

Quinn gathered his parchments together into a neat pile, put the corks back in his ink pots and flung the door open, ready to go and see what the watch had spotted.

Behind him, he could hear Kurt muttering as he dragged himself to his feet.

Half of Quinn hoped he took a very long time to join them, even as the other half wanted to race back, scoop up all his parchments and writing tools and take them on deck with him.

For a moment, Quinn dithered in the passageway, but then Jericho shouted again and he pushed Kurt out of his mind.

Ash was right. What could he do?

~

Quinn hadn't expected the edge of the world to be so crowded. As he stood on the sandy road, swaying slightly after so many weeks on the rolling deck of the *Libertas*, he was jostled once, twice, a third time by people pushing past him.

"Move, Quinn!" Ash shouted in his ear, dragging him by the elbow to the side of the road.

"I've never seen so many people," he said, shaking his head, his ears assaulted by a babble of voices. The "port to port side" that Jericho had spotted from the watch was teeming.

"Sure you have!" she said with a laugh. "It's just like market day at King Orel's castle – but you're not used to it anymore!"

It was true, Quinn reflected, taking a closer look. There were scores of people going about their business, but no more than he had seen on a busy day in Oakston, the capital of Verdania. But after four moon cycles at sea with only the crew for company, people – particularly in large numbers – were a novelty.

Quinn blinked as a wooden handcart rumbled past, whipping dust into his eyes.

"Come on, Quinn," said Ash, tugging his arm again. "We'll get left behind."

He followed in her wake, stomach growling in anticipation. Enticing aromas of smoky, grilling meats were wafting their way from a row of food stalls on one side of the port. He could see steaming pots over open fires and, at the other end of the stalls, a display of brightly colored fruits and vegetables – yellow, red, green and . . . was that purple?

As Ash strode ahead of him, Quinn was struck by how alike they looked these days, both small and wiry with dark hair. She had freckles and blue eyes. His skin had turned a deep brown over the months they'd spent at sea, so that it was almost the same color as his own hazel eyes. But other than that, they could be twins.

Skinny twins.

Keeping a wary eye out for Gelynions, Quinn took in the squat structures that lined the teeming port, which seemed hastily constructed around the deep, natural harbor. He slowed to a halt as another handcart cut across his path, and swiped at a bead of sweat running down his nose. It was only early, but the clammy heat of the day was already creeping up and up. On board the *Libertas*, with the ocean breeze sweeping the deck, Quinn had been aware of rising temperatures (and marked them in his notes), but it was only once they'd stopped in port that he'd realized just how warm this part of the world was.

"Come on, Quinn, what are you doing?" shouted Ash, pushing her way back through the crowd towards him. "Zain's over there. And so is the *food*."

Quinn laughed. Ash's plant knowledge didn't only extend to making colored inks – she'd learned some herb craft from her mother, Sarina, before her mother's death, and she was constantly muttering about the fact that the *Libertas* crew were a very lean bunch now, and that undernourished bodies never healed as well. Quinn tended to put this in the basket labeled "things too big to worry about." There wasn't much they could do about their supplies situation except to stock up, and eat up, when they could.

Today was going to be an "eat up" kind of day.

The closer they got to the stall, however, the more apparent it became that Zain wasn't happy. Then again, Quinn thought, cheerful wasn't really a word one associated with Zain. Imposing, perhaps. Or terrifying . . . But Quinn knew it was mostly just his appearance that gave that impression. Mostly.

"You three stay close to me," Zain had told them before they'd disembarked. Quinn had watched enviously as Dilly, Ison, Abel and Jericho had hustled down the gangplank and disappeared into the crowd, with Zain's "be back in two bells or else!" ringing in their ears.

"Couldn't Ash and I just . . ." he'd begun, hoping he and Ash might get the chance to scout around on their own for a while.

"No," said Zain. "I need the mapmaker to make the map, remember? You stay with me."

Strange, thought Quinn, how Zain suddenly remembered the importance of the mapmaker when they were in this exciting, bustling port, and yet he'd

15

had no qualms about dispatching Quinn into a deserted, forbidding tribal village . . .

"It's a lot easier to hide a Gelynion horde in a crowd," said Zain, as though reading Quinn's mind. "Besides, I may need your help with languages."

Quinn had nodded. He could understand the basics of several different languages, including his own, Renz, Athelstanish, Gelynion and, perhaps most useful, Suspite, the language at the heart of all others. He'd also picked up Deslondic, simply from eavesdropping on the crew's conversations. His talent for languages had proved handy on their journey so far.

And it's about to be tested again, thought Quinn now, taking in the situation at a glance. The stall keeper did not understand Zain's attempts to order food.

"You try," Zain commanded in a low voice, turning to Quinn.

"Okay," said Quinn, sweating profusely in the hot sun, feeling the press of people behind him. There wasn't a breath of wind and the air seemed to settle around him like a fine mist.

"Good morning, good sir," he tried in Suspite. Nothing.

"I already tried that," hissed Zain in his ear, clearly not enjoying the closeness of the heat and crowd any more than Quinn was. "And Deslondic."

You could have said, thought Quinn, before trying again in Renz. Then Gelynion. Then Athelstanish. In desperation, he even tried the series of clicks and vowel sounds that had made up the language in the tribal village. Nothing.

Quinn blew the hair off his face in exasperation, as the crowd behind them grew restless with their efforts and began to shout orders over their heads. Zain nudged Kurt beside him, and Kurt muttered a few words in his clipped Northern dialect. The stall keeper shook his head again – at which point, Zain threw his hands up and ushered the group off to one side of the stall, out of the crush.

"We might have to resort to sign language," Quinn said. "Or try a different stall?"

"Or you could try Verdanian," said Ash, watching the proceedings from beside him.

Quinn laughed. "I'm pretty sure these people will never have heard Verdanian in their lives," he stated.

"Okay," she said, mildly. "Only, they don't look surprised to see us." She waved her arm in the general direction of the throng. "We're the only ones here who look like us, in breeches and tunics, and nobody cares."

Quinn stared. She was right. Most of the people around them were obviously locals, their skin a beautiful caramel color, their hair dark and straight. Males and females both wore soft, knee-length cotton tunics in bright colors and looked, to Quinn, whose breeches felt hotter and heavier by the minute, cool and comfortable.

A few looked different, some dark skinned like Zain and the other Deslonders, while others looked as though they'd made their way down from a tribal village in the north, similar to the one the Verdanians had "visited." But no one was paying any attention at all to Quinn, Ash and Kurt, who were the odd ones out in this crowd.

"Also," Ash added conversationally, "nobody's tried to kill us. I think they've seen Verdanians before – and liked them, which, to me, rules out a brief visit from Dolan or Odilon."

Quinn laughed again; he couldn't imagine the other Verdanian crews leaving a good impression either. He looked to Zain, who nodded his head, and they pushed their way back to the stall counter.

Without much hope, Quinn tried his greeting in Verdanian.

"Ah, Verdania!" said the stall keeper in delight. "Yes, yes!"

Zain and Quinn exchanged looks. "You know Verdanian?" said Zain, carefully.

"Yes, yes!" said the stall keeper, with a big smile. "My friend, he taught me."

Quinn's eyebrows flew up. "Friend?" he asked.

"Yes," said the stall keeper. "My friend, Mr. Frey."

"Your friend is Verdanian?" asked Zain, looking as perplexed as Quinn felt. How could a Verdanian man have ended up here? As far as Quinn knew, no Verdanian had ever been this far west. And, until they'd been sent on this crazy quest to map the world, no Verdanian would have even known this place was here.

"Yes," said the stall keeper, nodding so enthusiastically that his bright-red robes rippled beneath him. "You must meet him! Come with me now!"

With that, he walked away from his counter. "Wait!" shouted Zain. "Let us buy supplies first. Then we will come."

Not for the first time, Quinn thanked the stars that his captain was a practical man. As interested as he was in meeting this mysterious Verdanian, he was far more interested in filling his grumbling stomach.

Having spent a lot of time hungry, Quinn knew that everything was easier on a full stomach.

Chapter Two

Mr. Frey had been away from Verdania for a long time. Quinn took in the man's wild, graying hair, his long, grizzled beard, and his deep-yellow robes. His callused feet were bare, his hands large and rough, and his face blank.

The most telling sign of his long-term residency in this steamy port, however, stood beside him. Frey had one arm around a dark-haired woman, and the other around a tall, lanky boy of about Quinn's age, who looked to be his son.

The stall keeper was excitedly explaining to Frey, in a mix of Verdanian and the local language, the sudden appearance of a party of strangers at Frey's front door. They all stood awkwardly in the dust just behind him, with chickens pecking around their feet, and a large black dog growling at them from its tense, crouched position near the door. So far it hadn't moved towards them, but Quinn had no doubt that one word from Frey would have it hurtling across the porch, teeth flashing.

Frey nodded as the stall keeper finally wound down. "Thank you, Michel," he said in Verdanian, as a courtesy to the listening visitors, Quinn supposed. "It is indeed always good to see faces from home."

Ash shifted beside Quinn. "And yet he looks so unhappy to see us," she whispered so that only Quinn could hear. Quinn knew what she meant; he was beginning to wish he'd gone back to the *Libertas* with Cook, Kurt and the supplies. He was also regretting eating quite so much of the stall keeper's delicious grilled beef in flatbread, which was starting to roil in his stomach.

"We were not expecting to see a Verdanian face so far from Verdania," said Zain, calmly. "How did you come to be in this place?"

Frey paused, and Quinn could see his grip tighten on the shoulders of the woman and the boy.

"I could say the same of you," he said, tightly. "But there is a time to share stories, and that is once we know each other a little better. Come, come . . ." He gestured towards the dark interior of the hut behind him. "Let us drink and talk."

He ushered the woman and boy through the door before him, gesturing to Michel to stay outside. Quinn was glad to be following Zain's bulk down the dusty path, past the growling dog on the porch and into the dark, cool interior.

Once inside, he looked about with interest. From the outside, the smooth, brown hut had looked small, but he could see that this impression had been misleading. It opened up into one large room, with a high ceiling, all smoothed off with the same material as the hut's exterior. Surreptitiously, Quinn ran his hand along the wall, and was surprised to find that it felt the same as his mother's earthenware jug. The interior walls were painted white, much like his own cottage in Markham, but there the resemblance ended, because here lightweight woven rugs embellished with sparkling beads added splashes of vibrant color on the floors, on the chairs, and over the dark wooden table. Quinn's eye was caught by a particularly vibrant shade of the deepest blue and he nudged Ash.

She nodded, eyes narrowed, and Quinn knew she was making a mental note to try to find out how that color was made. He hoped she did. He'd like that shade in his ink palette.

The group arranged itself around the low-set furniture, with Zain opting to sit cross-legged on the cool, tiled floor. Quinn supposed this was more comfortable for him than trying to squeeze his huge frame onto a low chair. Or perhaps he was worried that the wooden slats slung with what looked like cow hide wouldn't support his weight. Quinn smothered a smile at the thought of the dignified Zain crashing through a chair . . .

"Keila, make us tea, please," said Frey. "No, wait. Bring *cacao*."

The woman nodded and left the room. "Keila is my wife," Frey was saying, "and this is Tomas, our son."

The watchful boy, sitting next to his father, nodded.

"They both speak Verdanian," Zain noted.

"Yes," said Frey. "I taught them. And Michel. To remind me of what I'd left behind, and to remind Tomas of his heritage."

From the expression on Tomas's face, Quinn got the impression that the Verdanian lessons hadn't been the highlight of his day, but Quinn, for one, was happy that everyone could understand what was going on. It took the pressure off him.

"Ah yes," said Zain, as Keila reentered the room carrying a wooden tray on which rested an earthenware jug and what looked like six delicate pottery mugs. "Your heritage. Perhaps you could tell us a little of your story. As I said, we are surprised to find you here in this far-flung corner of the world."

Frey took a mug from his wife and she poured steaming brown liquid into it. A sweet, earthy scent filled the air. Quinn sniffed deeply. If it tasted half as good as it smelled, he was looking forward to trying this *cacao*.

"Well," said Frey. "Perhaps you could tell me first how you come to be here."

23

Zain, face impassive, outlined their journey, leaving out details about the King's prizes, and the fact that Quinn was the mapmaker. Quinn wondered why his captain was being so cagey – but then he remembered that Zain's caution in Kurt's village had probably saved all their lives.

"I see," said Frey, drinking deeply. "My story is much more . . . accidental, I suppose you would say."

Quinn reached eagerly for his mug as Keila handed it to him, and took a sip. The taste of the *cacao* filled his mouth, coating it with a bitter sweetness unlike anything he'd ever experienced. He looked over at Ash, who was rolling her eyes with pleasure as she drank it straight down.

"Ah, you like the *cacao*," said Frey. "One of my favorite things about living here . . . But there is so much I miss about Verdania. The green, rolling hills. The four seasons. The way the days seem to dissolve into the evenings, which evaporate into the deepness of night. Here, in Barbarin, it is always hot and wet, and it is either day, or it is night, as though someone has pulled down a black curtain . . ."

Frey stared down into his empty mug, lost in thought. The room was silent. Quinn sipped the last of his drink, filing away the name of this place, and wondered why a man who missed Verdania so much didn't return home.

Zain had the same thought, and voiced it.

"Ah, well," said Frey. "I can't go back. It is a long journey, as you know. And I don't even know the way. There is no map."

Zain shook his head. "But you got here in the first place. Surely you know where you are?" Quinn noticed that he'd barely touched his drink. He wondered if there was any chance Zain would hand him the leftovers . . .

Frey exhaled, and stood, pacing around the back of his seat. Keila moved to sit beside Tomas, holding his hand.

"Sometimes a journey is not as straightforward as one might hope," was all Frey would say.

Zain said nothing. Quinn had noticed that his captain used silence to great effect. When faced with that impassive expression and an ever-deepening hole of quiet, people rushed to fill it by saying something, anything. Quinn knew he'd fallen into that trap more than once.

Frey was no different. "I left Verdania twenty years ago with a group of, er, friends," he said. "Unfortunately, we ran into a storm and capsized. By sheer luck, I washed up on an island, where I stayed for a long time, living on local fruits and rainwater. One day, I spotted a boat that rescued me and brought me here."

Zain thought for a while. "Why here?" he asked.

"Keila's father was the captain of that boat," said Frey, reaching down to rest a hand on his wife's shoulder. "He was a fisherman, looking for new grounds."

25

"But . . ." said Quinn, not realizing he was voicing his thoughts aloud, "we're on the wrong side –"

"Ignore my young friend," said Zain, smoothly interrupting before Quinn could finish his thought. Quinn shook his head, annoyed at himself. Just because he carried a map of their journey in his head didn't mean that anyone else needed to know that. Quinn knew they'd traveled from the east side of this strange land, around the top to the west, which made Frey's story implausible. Keila's father would have had to travel from the west coast to the east coast to rescue Frey. Quinn wasn't entirely sure of the layout of this end of the coastline, but by anyone's calculations it was a very long way for a fisherman to go just to find new fish.

"Ah, yes," said Frey, giving Quinn a strange look. "Anyway, I ended up here and here I stayed."

"And the others in your party?" asked Zain, politely.

"All gone," said Frey, shaking his head in sorrow. "Lost when our boat overturned."

"That is, indeed, unfortunate," said Zain. He stood up. "Well, it has been a pleasure to see a familiar face so far from Verdania," he said. "And now, we have our supplies and will be on our way."

Frey looked relieved. "You will leave today?"

"Indeed," said Zain, while Quinn tried to hide his disappointment. He would have liked some time to have a good look around this place. It was a large, well-settled village, a trading center by the looks of things. There was much to be learned here.

"Thank you for the *cacao*," said Ash to Keila. "I've never had anything so delicious." She, too, looked disappointed to be leaving – though whether that was because of the *cacao* or that deep-blue dye, Quinn was unsure.

"You must take some," said Keila, rushing out of the room once more and returning quickly with two small clay jars. "Here," she said, proffering them to Ash. "*Cacao* – and some *indican* . . . I noticed you admiring the blue rugs."

"Oh, thank you," said Ash, who looked as though she was going to step forward and hug the woman – until she remembered she was a boy. "Er, thanks."

Now Frey was ushering them out of the cool room and into the harsh afternoon light. Quinn blinked, blinded momentarily by the change.

Zain nodded a brief good-bye, before striding off the porch and up the dusty path, scattering the chickens, which clucked angrily after him. Quinn waved awkwardly at Frey and his family before following, Ash behind him, clutching her precious jars to her chest.

"Is it just me," Quinn said, as they hurried after Zain, "or was that the strangest house visit you've ever attended?"

"I'm beginning to think that social skills aren't Zain's strong point," Ash said with a laugh. "This is the second time we've scarpered away from someone's front door."

"Exactly," said Quinn, quickening his step. "And last time there was a very good reason."

Ash nodded. "So you're wondering what the reason might be this time?"

Quinn didn't respond. He was too busy sorting through the pictures in his mind, trying to see what had raised Zain's suspicions.

Whatever it was, he had a feeling they'd be seeing Mr. Frey again.

~

It was Cleric Greenfield who provided the answers they needed. Zain, Quinn and Ash had arrived back at the *Libertas* to find it buzzing with activity, as all hands helped to stow the new supplies. Cook was already in the galley, planning a feast for the evening meal, and the other crew members were in high spirits after their shore visit. Dilly and Ison had even managed to buy themselves each a set of robes like the locals wore – Dilly's in red, Ison's in yellow – and were parading about the deck in them.

But Jericho had news. He'd spotted the *Fair Maiden*, Odilon's ship, easing into the crowded port not two bells prior. Quinn and Ash had both yelped in excitement, for the *Fair Maiden* meant Ajax, Odilon's mapmaker and their friend. Zain had laughed at their enthusiasm. "Does this mean that you've forgiven him for stealing your rug?" he asked Quinn.

"Well, as it was you who pointed out that he needs it more than I do, it would be churlish of me to hold it against him, don't you think?" responded Quinn, impishly.

Now that Ajax was here, Quinn was just looking forward to seeing his red-haired friend again. As was Ash, if her blush was anything to go by.

Before they could go in search of him, however, there was the small matter of Frey to be discussed.

"Frey is hiding something," said Zain, when Quinn asked him why their visit had been cut short. "A man does not wind up in a place like this without reason. Particularly a Verdanian man. For all intents and purposes, we are beyond the end of the world as far as Verdanians are concerned."

He was right. Most Verdanians believed that the world ended at Verdanian borders, and that anyone who sailed much farther than that would go right over the edge.

Frey and his friends must have had a very good reason to get into a boat and sail away from Verdania.

"Frey, did you say?" said Cleric Greenfield, in his ponderous way, as he walked past. "Not Freyne?"

"He said Frey," said Zain. "But why do you ask about Freyne?"

"Only because he is one of the most notorious thieves ever to have graced Verdania," said Cleric Greenfield, wrinkling his already wrinkled nose. "He was suspected of stealing pieces of King Orel's mother's court jewelry right out from under the noses of the palace guards. Some rubies and emeralds and, of course, the famed loganstone set."

Quinn gasped. He'd never actually seen a loganstone, but he'd heard about them: the most precious stones in Verdania were a deep, burnished yellow, the color of the harvest moon, and found only in one secret location in the wilds of the West Country.

"Ah," said Zain. "What happened to Freyne?"

"That's just it," said the cleric. "Nobody knows. He was brought into the castle dungeons for questioning but he disappeared, along with six other desperate men."

"Indeed," said Zain quietly. "How do you know about him, cleric?"

"Well," said the old man, "as you know, I was one of the King's most trusted clerks for many years. I wrote and copied many of the court documents – until my eyes grew too tired. But I remember that particular story well, although it has been more than twenty years . . . Around the time you came to Verdania, Zain."

There was an uncomfortable pause while the cleric considered the passage of time and Quinn wondered whether Zain wanted to remember his first days in Verdania, after his capture during the Crusadic wars.

"And the stones were never found?" Zain prompted.

"No," the cleric said, with a rueful shake of his head. "Most unfortunate."

30

Zain clapped the cleric on the shoulder gently, though it still gave the older man a start. "Thank you, cleric, you have been most helpful," he said.

Cleric Greenfield smiled. "Right, well, I'll be off then, but I'll be seeing *you* later," he said to Quinn with a huge wink, as he wandered away.

Quinn tried to look innocent as Zain eyed him closely. "Why will the cleric be seeing you later?" Zain asked.

"He's just helping me with some . . . calculations," said Quinn. He was still not ready to tell anyone about his secret map. Zain nodded, apparently satisfied, and Quinn breathed a sigh of relief.

"Do you think that Frey is really Freyne?" asked Quinn, eager to direct the conversation away from his map in the cleric's cabin. "He may still have the loganstones!"

"I will think on this," said Zain, to Quinn's disappointment. "Much is at stake, and we mustn't act hastily."

"But imagine how happy King Orel would be if we returned with those stones!" said Quinn. "We'd win the 'treasure' section of the race in a snap – and, face it, we're not doing terribly well in that department at this stage."

The Race Around the World had two components: the winner would be the explorer who returned to Verdania within one year with the best map. But additional treasure would be looked upon favorably . . .

Zain chuckled. "Ah, Quinn, so impetuous. It is not just the treasure at stake here. There is the small question of what to do about Frey. Do we simply take the stones – if indeed any are left – and leave him here? Or must we return him with us to Verdania to face up to his actions? In which case, we must house him aboard the *Libertas* for many long months – and feed yet another unwilling passenger."

They both turned to look at Kurt, who was lolling on the deck, watching as everyone else worked hard in the hot sun. "We could always just make a swap," said Quinn hopefully. "Kurt wouldn't go hungry here."

Zain chuckled again. "You are very keen to offload that boy," he said. "And yet he has done nothing to you."

"Not yet," muttered Quinn, darkly. He wouldn't have simply dumped Kurt on an isolated beach, but here, where there were people, and food, and possibilities, well . . . "He just makes it so clear that he thinks we're all beneath him."

"We do not know his full story," said Zain.

"Only because he hasn't deigned to tell us," replied Quinn, hotly.

Zain held his hand up. "But what we do know is bad enough . . ."

Quinn rolled his eyes. Zain was going to go through the loss of Kurt's parents again, and Quinn did feel sorry for the boy about that. But he was still wary.

"Okay," he said, wearily. "But I don't have to like him."

Zain's laugh boomed across the deck. "No, Quinn Freeman. No, you do not. And now, I will go and think on what to do about Frey – and I believe there is a certain redhead waiting for your attention over there on the dock."

Quinn turned to follow Zain's pointing finger and there was Ajax, hopping up and down at the bottom of the gangplank, waving wildly, grinning that huge, infectious smile of his. He'd lost a little weight, Quinn noticed, but other than that looked as healthy as ever.

"We can go?" Quinn asked. "I thought you were worried about losing your mapmaker."

"I have looked around now, all seems safe enough," said Zain. "But be back by four bells. You heard what Frey said. The night comes suddenly here, and it will not do to be lost in the dark."

Quinn shivered. No, that wouldn't do at all.

Chapter Three

Lying on their backs in the shade, Quinn, Ash and Ajax watched the local children playing on the banks of the wide, deep-green river they'd discovered behind the port. The game seemed to consist of running, throwing themselves onto one of the heavy vines that hung from the tall, dense trees above them, and flinging themselves into the water with a resounding splash.

Quinn lazily contemplated removing his boots and shirt and having a turn, but it seemed like too much effort.

The trio had settled instantly back into their comfortable friendship. *Almost* instantly. Ajax had been sheepish when Quinn had run down the gangplank to greet him, worried about what Quinn might say about the missing rug, but Quinn had quickly assuaged his worries.

"You found it too," he reminded Ajax – as Zain had reminded *him*.

"I know," said Ajax, "but I should have said something. It was a last-minute thing – I couldn't face Odilon with nothing."

"Even after he'd left you behind at the tribal village," said Ash, wryly.

"He's the captain," said Ajax, simply. "I'm just the mapmaker. Mind you, my absence didn't hurt – he seems to have realized that he needs me to win the race."

Quinn laughed. "That took long enough."

"Yes," agreed Ajax, with a grin. "He keeps walking around muttering 'can't win without the mapmaker.'"

Which was odd, Quinn reflected, but he didn't have time to think about it as his friends had run off through the port and he'd hurried after them.

Now, the angle of the sun told him it was nearing four bells, and time to begin making their way back to the ship. Their explorations had taken them far from the port, beyond the edges of town, which was bordered on two sides by the ocean and the wide river. Frey had called it Barbarin, though whether that was the port or the whole land, Quinn wasn't sure. He made a mental note to ask someone, and write it on his map. A place with a name seemed less hostile than one without.

The one dusty road branched off into a tumble of rundown huts on the fringes of the port, before punching straight out through the dense trees, which seemed to hover on the fringes, ready to push back on the town at the first opportunity.

They had followed the road out of town and discovered that it led to another, smaller outpost. Quinn wanted to cross the empty road between the two while the light was still with them.

"Oh, Quinn," said Ajax, suddenly. "I nearly forgot. I've got something to show you."

"Okay," he said to Ajax, "but you'd better make it quick. I don't want to be out here in the dark."

Ajax laughed. "That's right – you're not a fan of the dark, are you?"

"Hmph," said Quinn. "No more than you are of heights . . . or spiders."

Ash rolled over in the lush grass to look up at them. "Are you quite finished comparing fears – or can we see whatever it is that Ajax has to show you?"

Quinn wanted to "hmph' again but, given that Ash had no apparent fears, there was nothing more to say.

"It's this," said Ajax, reaching deep into his pocket and pulling out a crumpled piece of parchment.

Quinn winced, seeing the precious vellum treated so carelessly, but held out his hand to take it. "It's one of your drawings," he said, looking at the neat, sure strokes of ink.

"I've been using that notebook that Master Blau gave us to draw pictures," said Ajax. "I'm not as good with words as you are, Quinn, so it's the easiest way for me to keep a record of the journey. Do you know this man?"

"It's Odilon," said Quinn, recognizing Ajax's captain without difficulty, due to Ajax's drawing skill. "And . . ." He paused, looking closely at the other man depicted in the drawing. He would recognize that impressive moustache anywhere. "Juan Forden!" exclaimed Quinn.

"I thought he might be Gelynion," Ajax said. "But I didn't see him. You know, before. That's why I drew him . . ."

Ajax had been on board the *Libertas*, readying her for a quick getaway, the last time Quinn had seen Juan Forden.

"What's he doing with Odilon?" asked Ash, sitting up to take a closer look at the drawing.

"I don't know," admitted Ajax. "I couldn't hear. I was on the *Fair Maiden*, and they met on the dock."

"They're here?" said Ash, round-eyed. "The Gelynions are *here* – in this port?"

"And you wait until *now* to bring it up?" said Quinn, jumping to his feet.

"Well, I forgot," mumbled Ajax. "I was so excited to see you two and then . . ."

Quinn knew that not everyone had his memory. But he failed to comprehend how anyone could forget seeing a boatful of Gelynions.

"Um, Quinn," continued Ajax.

Quinn had a feeling he wasn't going to like what was coming.

"It's, er, about, you know, your memory," said his friend. "I know you don't like to talk about it but, er, well, I *might* have let slip to Odilon about it."

Quinn stilled. "When you say *might* . . ."

"Well, you know he was there in the village when you did the language thing," said Ajax. "He asked me about it when I got back on board. I tried to laugh it off but then I made a joke about you just memorizing all those words to add to your collection of languages and . . . well, he didn't seem to find it funny. He went on a bit about unfair advantages."

Quinn swallowed. He didn't like the sound of this. Odilon, a courtier from King Orel's castle, was the richest explorer in the race, and – like Dolan, the third participant – he had a lot to lose if Zain won. First, there was the seat on the King's council that he'd nominated as his prize and, second, he would lose face if Zain, a slave, trumped him. Quinn wasn't sure which would hurt the haughty minor Lord the most.

If Odilon thought that Zain had an unfair advantage – namely Quinn – he would do what he could to even the competition. But how far would he go?

"We need to get back *now*," said Quinn, tucking the drawing into his pocket. "Zain will know what to do."

If nothing else, Quinn would feel much better in the company of his solid, sizeable captain.

As the trio turned back towards the port, Quinn watched one last little girl swing herself from the bank, up and over in a long, graceful arc to the center of the river. Her hair flowed behind her and her smile was as wide as a crescent moon as she let go and threw herself into the water. She looked so carefree, thought Quinn wistfully – a million miles from Gelynions and races and maps.

"Come on, Quinn," Ash called urgently, already on the path back to town.

Quinn waited one more moment, until the giggling little girl popped back to the surface, before trudging after his friends. His legs felt heavy and his heart even heavier.

He hadn't asked for any of this. He'd been happy at home, with his family and his books, spending time with Ash. Now he was who knew how far from the safety of Markham, and it seemed his memory was becoming less and less of a secret, and more and more of a problem.

Quinn's stomach churned with every step as he walked beneath the trees. The path was strewn with sticks and logs, and he had to watch where he put his feet. Ahead of him, he could see Ash's and Ajax's heads bent together, talking heatedly as they walked. Ajax also knew Ash's secret – that she was really a girl – and Quinn wondered if he'd managed to spill that to Odilon as well.

Now, though, they seemed to be discussing the health of the plant that Ash had given Ajax when they'd last met – and it didn't sound as though it was doing well. Just as Quinn was about to call out to them to wait up, a hand, clamped over his mouth from behind and dragged him back on his heels. "Don't move," a voice hissed in his ear.

Quick as lightning, Quinn dug both his elbows straight back as hard as he could, while biting down on the hand, feeling the skin squish between his teeth.

"Oof!" shouted the voice, as the hand dropped away. "You bit me!"

Pivoting on the balls of his feet, Quinn turned to face his assailant, who had doubled over, winded by the attack from Quinn's pointy elbows.

"Tomas?" he said, in disbelief. Frey's son, who'd said not one word during their entire meeting, was attacking him?

"Don't move," the boy gasped, trying to catch his breath.

"I don't think you're really in a position to give orders," said Quinn, loftily, already thinking about how he was going to relay this story to Ajax. His first real one-on-one fight! And he'd taken out his opponent with just his elbows and his teeth.

"Serpent!" said Tomas. "Behind you."

Serpent? Quinn had read about them in books, but there were no serpents in Verdania, so he'd never seen one.

He pivoted back and there it was. What he'd thought was a fat log poking out from the grass on the side of the track had moved – and exposed itself as a slithering black length of scales, topped by two red eyes and long white fangs.

"Wh-wh-what do we do?" he stammered, mouth dry, as the creature reared up to face them, exposing the smooth white underside of its body.

"Stand still," said Tomas, from the side of his mouth. "If it bites you, you die."

They both froze like statues; the snake continued to survey them, head waving from side to side, the rest of its thick body coiling out onto the track to join it. Quinn tried to guess its length and stopped counting at twenty paces – he didn't want to know anymore.

"We can't stay here all day," he whispered.

"We can't get past it, and we can't outrun it," Tomas hissed back. "So we stay."

"What do you normally do?"

"I'm not *normally* stupid enough to encounter one."

Tomas was very comfortable with the Verdanian language, Quinn noted, feeling his face burn.

"If you hadn't grabbed me, this wouldn't have happened," Quinn said, stung.

"If I hadn't grabbed you, you would have stepped on it! Now I'm beginning to wonder if I should have just left you to it. *Simplato!*"

Quinn didn't need to understand Barbarin to know he'd been insulted. He didn't lose his temper often, but this boy's attitude on top of his own worries meant a spectacular explosion felt imminent. He pushed his anger down, which simply added to the tight feeling in his stomach.

"Can we discuss this later?" Quinn said, through clenched teeth, thinking that he'd like to focus that discussion on exactly why Tomas was following him around, but it would have to wait. "We need to get out of here – I'm not particularly interested in becoming this thing's dinner." He gestured in the direction of the serpent, which immediately reared back, hissing and spitting.

"Don't. Move," Tomas repeated. "If you move, it will kill you."

"Right. Sorry."

As they stood there, in a frozen tableau, Quinn noted that the sun had dropped considerably towards the horizon.

"How much daylight do we have left?" he whispered.

Tomas paused, considering. "Not much."

Right. They needed a plan, and fast. If they waited for this creature to lose interest and wander away, they'd be standing here in the dark. The very black dark.

Quinn's mind raced, discarding one idea and then another. He looked into the dense grass on either side of the track. Could they run in there and hide? If they went in opposite directions, at least one would escape. *But it might not be you,* a little voice whispered in his mind.

Not that idea, then.

He gently blew the damp hair off his sweating forehead, eyes following it upward. And upward. To the thick vines that hung from the trees above them. He remembered the little girl swinging . . . "How high can you jump?" he muttered to Tomas.

"What?"

"Can you reach that vine?" He risked a tiny nod towards a strong-looking vine that hung an arm's length above their heads, a few paces ahead of Tomas.

"Maybe," the boy said, doubtfully.

"You'll only get one chance," said Quinn, with one eye on the serpent, which was becoming agitated, rolling its coils, scales flashing in the dying sun. "When I say 'go,' you need to jump forward, grab that vine and swing over the serpent."

"And then?"

"*Leif's boots!* And then *run!*"

Tomas thought for a few seconds. "Okay," he said, without moving.

Quinn eyed the distance to the vine he'd designated for himself. A little farther out than Tomas's, and considerably higher. He hoped all those jumps from the deck to the lower mast that Zain had been making him do were about to pay off. Looking at the fangs in front of him, the alternative didn't bear thinking about.

"Right," he whispered, taking a deep breath and tensing all over. "On three. One. Two. THREE!"

Using all his pent-up anger and frustration to fuel him, Quinn leapt up and out, feeling as though time slowed as he reached out with his fingers, desperately hoping he'd connect with that vine. He felt, rather than saw, the serpent move, a rush of speed beneath his feet, and then the smooth vine was in his hands. For a moment, it dipped under his weight and he froze, wondering if he was about to land *on* the serpent – but then he was swooping up, a listless, sticky breeze on his face.

Clutching the vine with both hands, Quinn drew his knees up for better clearance as he traveled over the serpent's long body, the momentum of its strike carrying it in the opposite direction. Out of the corner of his eye, he could see Tomas clinging to another vine, sailing beside him.

As the vine reached the zenith of its arc, Quinn leapt again, throwing his body forward, trying to use the motion of the swing to carry him as far down the track as he could. In the back of his mind, he could hear Zain's voice: "Stay on your feet, Quinn Freeman."

He landed, balls of his feet first, then heels, with his knees soft to help break the impact as Zain had taught him, and skidded slightly in the dust, arms cartwheeling to maintain his balance. Tomas landed in a heap beside him, letting out a startled yelp.

"That was elegant," Quinn joked, as Tomas scrambled to his feet. He hadn't forgotten the "stupid" comment.

"Yes, well, I usually land in water," said Tomas, as they took off.

"Will it chase us?" asked Quinn, breathing heavily in the humidity.

"I'm not stopping to find out."

With that, they put on an extra burst of speed and ran pell-mell to the end of the path – and straight into Ajax and Ash.

"Where have you been?" asked Ash, exasperated. "We looked around and you were gone."

"Can't stop," puffed Quinn. "Come on!" He was taking no chances while the serpent could still be behind them.

They ran as hard as they could until they reached the first huts of the outpost. Only then did they slow to look back.

"I don't think it followed us," said Tomas.

"What are we running from?" asked Ajax, whose fair skin was bright red with exertion. He wasn't training every day like Ash and Quinn, and long weeks at sea meant his body wasn't used to running.

"A serpent," said Quinn. "Massive."

Ash's eyes were round. "Really? What did it look like?"

"Terrifying," said Quinn, shortly. "Be glad you didn't see it."

Tomas laughed. "You think that's terrifying? Wait till you meet the *pescarn*."

"The what?" Ash looked worried.

"It's a fish," said Tomas, "about this big." He held up his pointer finger.

Ajax laughed. "Bit small to be terrifying."

Tomas shook his head, face serious. "You never meet just one of them," he said. "Always more, ten, twenty . . . and they will eat the flesh off your bones in minutes."

Ajax blanched. "So . . . if we meet one, what do we do?"

Tomas laughed again. "Avoid them. Never cross a low river in the dry season – they will be hungry. Swim at night as they eat during the day. And if you absolutely have to cross a *pescarn* river, you need a distraction. Throw in some meat and cross downstream, quickly."

"You're making it up!" Quinn said, examining him closely. "We've been watching kids throw themselves in the river just this afternoon."

"Am not!" said Tomas, fiercely. "The *pescarn* like the white water. Here the river is slow moving."

"Hmm," said Ash. "All very interesting, but what exactly are you doing here?"

"Saving his life," said Tomas, pointing to Quinn.

Quinn snorted. "Right," he said. "We'd still be standing there if it was up to you."

Tomas winced. "I just needed time."

Quinn didn't bother to reply. "You haven't answered the question. Why are you here? Were you following me?"

"I wanted just to talk to you," said Tomas, toeing the dirt.

"About what?"

"Verdania," said Tomas, looking up. "I wanted to ask you all about Verdania. William doesn't talk about it much and I . . ." His voice trailed away.

"You were curious," said Ash. "That's understandable."

Quinn, who had noted the use of Frey's first name, was not so sure. "So you weren't keeping an eye on us for your father?"

Tomas's gaze shifted to a point over Quinn's shoulder. "Well . . . he did ask me to see where you went, what you did, but I would have done it anyway."

"You're a spy!" said Ajax, looking as though he was ready to pick Tomas up by the scruff of the neck and return him to the serpent.

"It's okay, Ajax," said Ash, putting a hand on his arm. "What did he learn today? Nothing except the fact that you like to eat and Quinn likes to daydream."

Quinn thought about the drawing in his pocket. "Is that all you learned?" he asked Tomas.

"Yes! Well, no," the boy admitted. "I saw you passing something around, but I didn't understand what it was all about."

Quinn sighed. "We're going to need to take you to Zain," he said. "He'll want to talk to you."

He'd barely gotten the words out when Tomas hared off, disappearing into the gathering gloom between two huts before the Verdanians could even move.

"What do we do?" asked Ajax. "Chase him?"

"No," said Quinn, "He knows where he's going and we don't. Besides, it's getting dark and we've still got a fair way to go back to the dock. I say we get back to our ships and get out of here."

He'd had quite enough of this steamy port with its serpents and spies and thieves. Not to mention the possibility of Gelynions hiding behind every bush. The sooner he was safely back on board the *Libertas*, the better.

~

"Quinn, I don't have a freakish memory and even *I* know this is the third time we've seen that hut." Ash stopped dead in the shadows, pointing viciously at the offending hut. Pale light spilled from its small windows, and Quinn inhaled the delicious scent of frying onions as it drifted through the still night air.

"We're lost," Ash continued, voice flat.

"It all looks different in the dark," Quinn admitted. They'd been walking around in circles, through a sea of huts for what felt like days. The night had descended as suddenly as Frey had warned it would, and with it had gone their sense of direction. What made things worse was that all the locals, every man, woman and child, had disappeared indoors with the daylight, leaving the Verdanians feeling very alone.

Quinn wondered what was out here in the dark with them that made every single person feel the need to be inside. Perhaps that serpent had a lot of friends . . . He pushed that thought to the back of his mind.

"We need to knock on a door and ask for directions," said Ash, and not for the first time.

"No!" said Quinn and Ajax, in unison.

"Like I said before, we don't know who's behind the door," said Ajax.

"And, like *I* said before, we can't even speak the language," said Quinn. "Remember the stall keeper this morning? It wasn't until we pulled out Verdanian that we got anywhere. And there are about four people in this port who speak Verdanian."

Ash exhaled loudly. "Fine," she hissed. "We'll give it one more try. But if you don't get us back to the port this time, I am going to march up to the nearest door, bang on it and ask the way. Got it?"

"I'm sure it's this way," said Quinn, trying to sound confident as he led them off again into the unforgiving dark.

"That's what you said last time," said Ash, her voice tight with frustration.

They picked their way along a road, listening to the night noises around them. As they passed a hut, there'd be the low murmur of voices, the clanking of dishes in a kitchen, a child crying. Quinn froze as a dog barked deeply from a nearby porch, but it didn't seem to think they were worth leaving its station for.

As they continued down the road, the huts grew farther apart and Quinn's confidence rose. He remembered that when they'd left the crowded area around the port, there'd been a stretch of road through dense trees, and then the bulk of the town. Surely that's where they were now?

"I think we go down a bit farther, around a bend, and we should see the port ahead of us," he said to the others, his pace quickening. It was even darker here on this isolated stretch of road, and the deep black of the night sky seemed to press down from above. Ash hurried up beside him, and he felt her hand creep into his. He gave it a squeeze, faking a reassurance he did not feel, and she let go.

"Dark out here," said Ajax, and Quinn knew he was speaking just to hear a voice. And perhaps to drown out the rustling on other side of the road, as the night creatures went about their business. Most sounded small to Quinn, perhaps like the field mice or badgers at home, though there was a high-pitched, chattering sound out in the trees. Human? Animal? Ghost? Quinn wasn't going in there to find out. He picked up his pace.

Screeeeccch!

Quinn's blood froze at the sickening scream above his head, then he threw himself down onto the road, tasting dirt in his mouth. He felt a rush of air and risked a glance up, to see a large, dark shape with glowing yellow eyes flying overhead. In a heartbeat, it was gone.

"Leif's boots! Wha-a-at was that?" He sat up, brushing dirt off his face.

Ash and Ajax didn't answer, though strange noises were coming from their direction.

"Ash! Ajax! Are you okay?" He hurried to his feet and moved towards them in the dark . . . only to discover them doubled up in hysterical laughter on the side of the road.

"What's so funny?" he asked, indignantly. "I thought you were dying."

"We are," gasped Ajax. "Dying of laughter."

"Haven't you ever seen an owl?" Ash managed, between giggles. "I've never seen anyone hit the ground so fast."

"Oh, very funny," said Quinn, trying to shake dust out of his hair. "I've never heard one that sounded like that before – right on top of my head."

"Sorry," said Ash, sounding unrepentant. "It just looked so funny from behind you."

"*Hmph*," said Quinn. "Well, the show's over, and I'm hungry, so let's get going." He stomped off down the road, leaving them to follow – or not. His anger, and the thought of a hot meal on board the *Libertas*, was enough to give him an extra burst of speed. He could hear the other two trailing behind him.

"Quinn! Wait up!" said Ajax.

But Quinn had had enough. He was sick of wandering in the dark, sick of feeling scared and, frankly, sick of being surrounded by the unfamiliar. He walked faster, head down.

He reached the bend in the road that he'd remembered and paused momentarily to take in the faint, flickering lights of the port ahead of him. He could see the water in the distance, the lights from the ships at anchor reflecting off its ripples like twinkling stars. Unfortunately, the night sky above him remained stubbornly star free, and the thin sliver of the moon on the wane wasn't much use to light the road ahead, even without the tree cover. But at least he knew he was going in the right direction.

Quinn fingered the vellum in his pocket as he broke into a run. He wanted nothing more than to show Ajax's drawing to Zain – and hopefully turn the *Libertas* seaward immediately. The more distance he could put between himself, the Gelynions and Odilon, the better.

He was startled from his thoughts by shouting behind him. Quinn turned and peered back through the darkness, realizing that, in his grumpiness and haste, he'd lost sight of his friends. The sounds of scuffling, shrieking and muttered oaths rang clear on the night air, and Quinn hurried back around the bend in time to see Ajax and Ash being dragged into the trees by a group of men!

Dropping to a crouch, Quinn slid behind a shrub, thinking fast. Without a weapon, he couldn't rush up and release his friends. The best thing to do was to watch, wait and follow. But he needed to get closer.

He began creeping towards the group. Ash was putting up an almighty fight, thrashing and shouting, and almost breaking free of the short, thick man who had her by the arm. The group of four men had concentrated their efforts on containing Ajax, who definitely looked like the more difficult candidate for capture. But they hadn't reckoned on Ash's scrappy nature, Quinn thought with pride as he slid beneath the trees and into the shadows.

Unfortunately, she was no match for the strength of the man who held her – he simply picked her up, put her under his arm and pulled a knife on her. "Move again and I will cut you," he said. She stopped kicking, but Quinn thought that had more to do with the knife than the words – for the man had spoken Gelynion!

"So, Monstruo," the man continued, oblivious to the fact that Ash and Ajax had no idea what he was saying. "We have you now, little mapmaker."

Monstruo! Quinn sat back against the trunk of the nearest tree at the word. *Monstruo* meant "freak" in Gelynion – and it was the name they'd given *him*. The Gelynions had taken Ash, thinking that she was him!

He had no time to think about it now, though. The group had begun to move away from the road, deeper into the thick trees. Half of him wanted to run like crazy towards town to get Zain and the *Libertas* crew, but if he did that, he might never find this spot again.

Swallowing his fear, Quinn followed the wide trail they left, as close behind them as he could. Moist leaves slapped against his face in the dark, and he could hear rustling and scampering in the undergrowth as creatures ran from the unwieldy group ahead. His nose wrinkled at the damp, rotting smell that rose from the soft earth dislodged by his boots; his stomach churned.

Something slithered over his foot in the dark, and he froze, thinking of the huge serpent he and Tomas had outwitted. As he did, he realized the crashing sounds of the group moving through the undergrowth had stopped, and that he could hear voices – voices he recognized.

"Ah, you have both of them," said Juan Forden. "Well done. That makes three."

Three? Quinn tiptoed one tree closer to the voices, peering into the dark, trying to see what was happening ahead of him.

"Hmm," said a deeper voice, which Quinn knew instantly was Morpeth, Juan Forden's Deslondic "advisor." "The little one is even smaller than I remembered."

Forden laughed. "How can you tell in the dark? Put them with the other one."

Who was this "other one"? Quinn wondered. He crept even closer to the voices, hoping the combination of darkness and thick leaves helped to hide his white shirt. Sliding under a shrub, he pushed between the branches – and found himself staring into a small clearing, crowded with Gelynions. A small fire threw flickering light into the space, dancing against the dense walls of greenery on all sides. Forden stood in the middle of a group of ten or so men, talking heatedly, though Quinn couldn't make out the words. There was no sign of Ash or Ajax, though he noticed Morpeth on the opposite side of the clearing, staring fixedly down.

What was he looking at?

Quinn eased his way back, out from under the shrub and began making his way carefully around the clearing. He hoped the Gelynions were so busy listening to Forden that they wouldn't hear the odd stick snap. Overhead, that strange chattering noise began, shrieking and squawking. Quinn stopped dead, feeling his heart beat faster. He almost dropped to the dirt, like he had with the owl. Almost. Then he realized that the chattering, whatever it was, was the perfect cover for any noise he might make – and he needed to get out of that spot fast, in case the Gelynions came to investigate.

He burrowed through the undergrowth, nose close to the fetid earth, pushing and shoving. Behind him, he could hear the Gelynions crash into the trees, shouting and cursing, while the chattering overhead got even louder. He tried not to imagine what that horrible, non-human noise was, instead using it to propel him faster – away from the Gelynions.

In minutes, Quinn realized he was on the opposite side of the clearing. He slid forward on his stomach and once again found himself with a front-row view of proceedings. He could see Forden by the fire, shouting urgent orders into the trees. Morpeth must have gone with the other men to investigate the chattering noise, because he was nowhere to be seen. Quinn screwed up his eyes, trying desperately to see into the trees opposite. What was making that sound?

He saw what looked like little men jumping about up there, flinging sticks down through the branches.

He rubbed his eyes and peered again.

Nope, still there. But now that he looked more closely, he could see that the "little men" had long, curly tails, which they were using to cling to the tree branches, leaving their "hands" free.

Some kind of strange animal, then – and not one that Quinn wanted to see close up.

Time to get out of here.

Bringing his attention back to the clearing, he noticed a wide, dark space in front of him. Some kind of hole? He took another look at Forden, who was still alone in the center of the clearing, facing the chattering trees.

Taking a deep breath, Quinn crawled out on his stomach, feeling like one of the crabs that he and Ash had sometimes found at the river mouth in Markham.

Forden called out, and Quinn stilled, trying to sink deeper into the pungent soil, breathing hard.

It took him several seconds to realize that Forden's back was still to him. Quinn risked crawling forward another three paces, before stopping again. The chattering in the trees was almost deafening now, and he could barely hear the Gelynions shouting above the noise. He scrabbled forward the last few paces and peered down into the blackness of a wide, square pit . . .

Into three pale, scared faces.

Chapter Four

"Can you see them?"

Zain turned from his position against the ship's rail and looked down into Cleric Greenfield's worried face.

"No," he admitted. "I cannot."

"It's six bells," said the cleric. "They should have been back by now."

"Yes," said Zain. "I told them four bells." He cursed himself for becoming so distracted by his deliberations about Frey that he'd lost track of time. If nothing else, he'd been planning to find a shoemaker to repair the small hole that had begun to make its presence felt in the sole of his boot.

He turned back towards the port, no longer bustling as it was in daylight hours, but still busy enough.

"Aren't you going to look for them?"

Zain sighed. "Where would I begin?" he asked, as he

had asked himself many times since the four bells had rung. "They could be anywhere. Much better to wait here."

"Something must have happened," said the cleric, decisively. "They are –"

"Young," interrupted Zain. "As you reminded me not three days ago."

"Yes, but –"

"But nothing," said Zain, not wanting to show the cleric how worried he was beginning to feel. "I am sure they will turn up in good time."

"Hmph," muttered the cleric, sounding very much like Quinn. Zain suppressed a smile – those two were spending a lot of time together and it looked as though it was rubbing off on the good cleric.

"Where are you, Quinn Freeman?" Zain asked, staring out into the blackness behind the port. He had developed a soft spot for the plucky little scribe, though it would not do to let Quinn see it. Zain entertained himself briefly with thoughts of exactly what he would say to Quinn when the mapmaker did reappear.

"I'll give them one bell and then send a search party," he muttered to himself, mentally choosing crew members for the hunt. Jericho would want to go, he thought. And Abel. Ison, perhaps? And Kurt, he decided, though, thinking on it, he realized that it had been some time since he'd seen the Northern boy. Were the two together? It seemed unlikely.

"Stop! You can't go up there!"

Cleaver's voice, from the bottom of the gangplank, cut through Zain's thoughts.

"I can and I will!" was the gruff response, followed by the sounds of a scuffle.

Zain leaned over the rail. "Let Mr. Dolan aboard," he told Cleaver, eyeing his fellow explorer balefully. "Perhaps next time he will remember to ask permission."

Dolan appeared at the top of the gangplank, red faced and disheveled. "I don't need permission. Not to board a *slave's* ship."

"Yes," said Zain, deliberately. "You do. And if you continue to be discourteous, you will be marched back to the dock."

"You've got my mapmaker!"

"I've – what?" Zain's face turned to stone, as it always did when he wanted to hide his thoughts. It was a trick he'd learned in his earliest days in Verdania, and one that he'd perfected over many years.

"Ira Thornten! You've got him!"

"I see – and why would I want him?" parried Zain, mind racing. If Dolan's mapmaker was also missing, it put a whole new light on Quinn's absence. Particularly given that Ajax was with Quinn.

"Odilon told me you had him," blustered Dolan, looking less certain. "To hold me up. So much for our alliance."

"Indeed," said Zain, smiling faintly. "You put so much faith in our alliance that you are willing to march up here on the faintest excuse. I do not have your Ira. I'm perfectly happy with my Quinn."

"Well, where is he then?"

"Ira? I have no idea."

Dolan looked around suspiciously. "I don't see your mapmaker either."

"No, I seem to have . . . misplaced him as well."

Dolan stared at him. "What's going on?"

"That, my friend," said Zain, in a tone that was anything but friendly as he strode to the wheelhouse to retrieve his two-handed sword, "is what we're going to find out."

~

"Why are we here?" Dolan's face was ghostly in the pale flickering light.

"We will not find the boys without local knowledge," said Zain. "This man can help us."

They were standing on the porch of Frey's hut, waiting for someone to answer their knock. All was silent.

"He's not even here," said Dolan. "We're wasting our time."

"Oh, he's here," said Zain, loudly enough to be heard inside. "Or someone is. No one goes out and leaves candles burning. Mr. Frey is simply slow to respond. Isn't that right, Mr. *Frey?*"

The emphasis on Frey's name was deliberate. A heartbeat later, Zain heard movement behind the door – as he'd known he would. Freyne would have been bracing himself for this visit ever since Zain had first set eyes upon him.

Still, there was no sign of the door opening.

"This is a waste of time!" Dolan exploded. "We should be looking for them – now!"

"Perhaps you are right," Zain agreed. "Why don't you take your man and search that alley over there, while I wait for our host?"

Dolan raised an eyebrow at the suggestion but, after staring into Zain's uncompromising expression for a long moment, he nodded.

As soon as Dolan was out of sight, the door opened.

"You know who I am," said Frey.

Zain nodded.

Frey stepped forward, speaking so that only Zain could hear. "I won't go back."

Zain nodded again. "That is not a subject for discussion now. We need your help."

Surprised, Frey stepped back, allowing Zain to enter the room. The vibrant colors of the mats and throws were dimmed in the candlelight – but the sparkling beads that adorned them were dazzling, brought to life by the flickering glow.

"What's the problem?" asked Frey.

Zain noted that he'd moved to stand between his wife and his son, an arm around each. "We're looking for the boys that were with me today," said Zain, careful to keep Ash's secret. "Have you seen them?"

Frey laughed. "Not since you left."

Keila shook her head quickly. Tomas was slower to respond.

"Are you sure?" asked Zain, staring at the boy, who dropped his eyes. "Not even you, Tomas?"

"I – er." He stopped suddenly, and Zain noted his father's tight grip on the boy's shoulder. "No," Tomas finished.

"It's a shame," Zain continued, in a conversational tone, pacing the room, well aware of the impact his size had on others. "Because any help that we received from you in this matter would be looked upon . . . favorably."

Having given the matter of Frey long, hard thought, Zain had decided that he would not return him to Verdania. Frey had lived out the past twenty years in exile, and Zain knew what it cost a man to be so far from home for so long. The Verdanian, however, did not need to know of Zain's decision. Yet.

Frey looked up. "I don't know where they are," he said.

"But *you* do," Zain said, stopping in front of Tomas. "I don't need to know why, but I need to know where you last saw them."

The boy looked at his father, who nodded almost imperceptibly. "I can show you," said Tomas.

Zain exhaled with the relief that comes from a gamble that pays off. "I was hoping you might say that."

~

"Get us out of here!"

Quinn was so surprised to see Ira standing in a pit with Ash and Ajax that, at first, he didn't react to the noble boy's order.

"Where did *you* come from?" he whispered instead.

"Never mind that, you imbecile," hissed Ira. "It's wet down here. Get us out!"

Staring down into Ira's angry face, Quinn had one fleeting moment of fierce joy as he imagined simply walking away and leaving the blond boy down there, in the deep, dark, damp hole. But he pushed it aside – he'd never leave Ash and Ajax.

"Hmph," Ira went on, at Quinn's hesitation. "I should have known a simple *farm boy* couldn't be relied upon."

Quinn shook his head at the words. Ira had not gotten over the fact that Quinn had been chosen for the race ahead of Ira's friends Cedric and Norric.

"I'm not sure," Quinn retorted, surprising himself, "but I'm thinking that if I was down a hole and there was only one person here to save me I'd be a little more . . . polite to that person." There had been a time when Ira's haughty demeanor had intimidated Quinn, but not anymore. It wasn't working on Ash or Ajax either, judging by their suppressed chuckles.

"Oh, get on with it," Ira spat. "We haven't got time to play parlor games."

"Steady on," said Ajax, leaning in over the blond boy. "Quinn's doing his best."

"Quinn," Ira hissed, "is doing nothing – and I'd have thought speed was required here."

Quinn opened his mouth to reenter the slanging match, but realized that Ira was right. This wasn't the time.

Keeping one wary eye on Forden, Quinn scrabbled back into the trees, looking for something, anything, he could use to pull his friends out. The chattering sound up in the trees began again in a wave, growing louder and louder. Quinn glanced up, just to check that none of those little creatures were over *his* head.

Again, he noticed thick vines growing through the trees. Perfect for use as a rope! He reached up and with all his weight pulled down on a vine. It shifted, but did not break. He tried again, jumping up and wrapping his body around the greenery, trying to force it free.

Nothing.

He crawled back to the pit. "I need a knife," he said.

"Don't you have one?" Ira's disdain was palpable. Quinn winced. The knife situation was a sore point with him. Due to his family's finances, the Freeman boys did not receive a knife of their own until they were sixteen – which left Quinn more than a year short. Over the course of this journey, he'd collected three knives – and lost them all under circumstances that were beyond his control.

But he didn't have time to give Ira chapter and verse on all that.

"No," Quinn said, shortly. "And I'm thinking that yours hasn't done you much good." Ira's face told him that the shot had hit home. It was petty, Quinn knew, but he needed that small victory.

"You can have mine," said Ash, reaching down to her ankle, where she kept a kitchen knife strapped. "It didn't do me much good either." She held it up to hand it to Quinn, but he couldn't reach it, no matter how he stretched out.

"Let me try," said Ajax, holding the knife by the point and stretching up as far as he could to pass the handle to Quinn. He still couldn't reach.

"Oh for the love of –" Ira's oath was cut short as he grabbed the knife from Ajax and flung it up at Quinn, who had to duck as the sharp blade flew over his head.

"Also not a good idea to *kill* the person who's trying to save you," Quinn jibed.

"Just get on with it," said Ira, disagreeably.

Really, thought Quinn as he scrambled back into the trees and cut a length of vine, Ira was a hard person to help. He was relieved to note that Forden had left his position by the fire at last, and had moved to the other side of the clearing, yelling into the blackness at his hapless men, who were still trying to deal with those chattering creatures. From the shouts he could hear, it sounded as though the creatures were winning.

"Ash, you go first," he said, dropping the end of the vine over the edge of the pit and lowering it in. "You're the lightest and you can help me with the others."

"Got it," she said, giving the vine a light tug.

He tied the other end of the vine around his waist and began to pull, grunting as he took the strain of her weight. Moments later, Ash's head appeared over the top of the pit.

"I've never been so happy to see you," she said cheerfully, pulling herself up.

Quinn managed a smile through his grimace.

"Now what?" she said, standing beside him

"Now we –" He broke off as Forden suddenly turned back into the clearing. Grabbing Ash's arm, he pulled her down to the ground and dragged her back into the cover of the trees. Sweating, he watched as Forden returned to the fire, muttering to himself.

"Do you think you can find your way back to the road?" he whispered in Ash's ear. "Go back around the clearing and head directly north. You guys left a pretty obvious trail for me to follow, so I'm thinking you can find it."

She nodded, eyes wide and white in the darkness.

"Take this," Quinn continued, handing her Ajax's drawing. "Find Zain. Town is just around the next bend."

"What are you going to do?"

"I'll drag Ajax and Ira out and we'll follow you," he said, crossing his fingers in the darkness where she couldn't see. "Now hurry!"

She nodded and crawled off through the undergrowth. Quinn realized he still had her knife. He slid it down into his boot, hoping she wouldn't need it.

Peering through the trees, he noted that Morpeth had left the men in the trees, and returned to the fire with his captain. The two were deep in conversation.

Quinn hesitated. The Gelynions could look over at the pit at any time and, lying on top of it, he'd stand out like one of his brother Allyn's pimples. On the other hand, every minute he waited was one minute closer to *all* the Gelynions returning to the clearing – and who knew what would happen to Ira and Ajax then.

He gathered up his length of vine and, moving as quietly as he could, crept back to the edge of the pit on his stomach. "Ajax?" he said. "Are you ready?"

"Oh no," said Ira. "No way! I'm next. If you get him out, you're likely to leave me here."

"Don't be ridiculous," said Ajax. "As if Quinn would do that."

Quinn tried to look as though the thought had never crossed his mind.

"But you can go next," continued Ajax. "Quinn will need your help to get me out."

It was true. There was no way that Quinn could pull Ajax out by himself.

"If you stand on my shoulders," said Ajax to Ira, "it will make it easier for Quinn. Not as far to pull your weight."

Quinn heard grunting from below and then Ira's face was just over an arm's length from the top of the pit. "Go on, then," Ira said. "Throw me the vine."

Quinn did, maintaining his flat posture, and wrapping the vine around one wrist as he held it tight with both hands. He didn't want to risk standing with Forden and Morpeth so close. He felt Ira tug the vine, then his arm was nearly pulled from its socket as he took the blond boy's weight. He felt his body slide forward, and he dug his toes into the dirt, desperately trying to find solid purchase. Inch by inch he pulled at the vine, and finally Ira's hands appeared at the top of the pit, then his elbows and, finally, his head and chest, as he levered his way over the edge. Quinn relaxed as Ira climbed out, the weight coming off the vine, and he slowly got to his feet.

Suddenly, there was a huge tug on the vine as Ira pulled Quinn towards him. Quinn slid forward, feet scrabbling in the dirt. The next thing Quinn knew, two hands were shoving him in the middle of the back and he was falling . . .

"What are you –?" he shouted.

Quinn didn't even finish the sentence before he went over the top of the pit, face-first, down into the dark. A heartbeat later, he landed with an *oof* on something soft, and then the vine snaked down on top of him.

"That went well," moaned Ajax, from underneath him.

"Didn't it though," came Ira's smug voice from the top of the pit.

"You pushed me in!" Quinn said, fear and anger making his voice squeaky.

"Hmm," said Ira. "Maybe I did, and maybe you're just inept. But it's you those Gelynions are after, not me. With you down there, they won't go looking for me."

"What about your precious alliance?" Quinn managed, almost unable to speak, so great was his rage. It had been Dolan who had suggested they team up against the Gelynions. Quinn had never wanted to be part of it, deeming those on the *Wandering Spirit* "enemends" – but now he thought he'd shorten that to straight "enemies."

"Well now," said Ira, "was it not *your* captain who refused to show us your map at the time, saying something about being competitors?"

The rush of anger Quinn felt at Ira's sneering tone nearly knocked him off his feet. The noble boy was firmly in the camp that Zain, as a slave, should not have been allowed to join the race. Quinn, of course, remembered Zain's words: "We will fight as Verdanians against the Gelynion threat, but we compete only for ourselves."

Personally, Quinn thought this was more the former situation than the latter, but when he looked up to tell Ira, the pale circle of his face had disappeared.

"Ira!" Quinn hissed. "Ira!"

"It's no use," said Ajax, wriggling out from under him. "He's not going to come back."

"*Leif's boots!*" cursed Quinn.

Ajax managed a laugh. "How I've missed Leif and his boots," he said.

"Do you have something that better sums up our situation?"

"I can think of a few things, but I'm pretty sure your mam wouldn't be happy with any of them," said Ajax. "Perhaps we can while away the time coming up with some new curse words for you."

Quinn rolled his eyes. "This is no time for jokes."

"I don't know," said Ajax. "We're stuck in a hole in the middle of nowhere, in the dark, held captive by murderous Gelynions. If ever there was time for a joke, it's now."

"Ash will get help."

"Yeah, if Ira doesn't catch up with her first. He seemed pretty determined that the Gelynions should have you."

"Anything to win the race," said Quinn, morosely. He looked up at the patch of sky he could see through the mouth of the pit. More than ever he wished there was at least a friendly little star looking down on them. Maybe that way he wouldn't feel so abandoned. The walls of the pit seemed to press in even more closely.

"What's all that noise up there, anyway?" asked Ajax.

"Some kind of animals in the trees," said Quinn. "They don't seem to like the Gelynions."

"Neither do I, much," said Ajax.

"I wonder what they're doing out here," said Quinn. "It seems strange that they'd bring you all here rather than just taking you aboard their ship."

"I don't know," said Ajax. "I couldn't understand a word they were saying."

"And where did Ira come from?"

"Oh, that I know. They arrived in port this afternoon. He got off the *Wandering Spirit* to stretch his legs and wandered up the wrong alley."

"The Gelynions found him?"

"He reckons they were looking for him. He also told us a very long story about how he'd nearly fought off five of them by himself . . . but I got bored in the middle of that and didn't listen very closely."

"Hmm," said Quinn, thinking hard. All three mapmakers had been rounded up after Odilon had met with Juan Forden. Which made no sense at all. If Odilon had been looking for an advantage in the race, why would he have set Ajax up to be captured as well?

Unless . . .

"It's like the Gelynions are waiting for someone," said Quinn, slowly. "But who?"

He felt Ajax shrug in the darkness beside him, then stilled as a loud voice spoke above them.

"We should just kill them and go."

Quinn shrank down into the bottom of the pit at Forden's voice. Ajax, who couldn't understand Gelynion, followed a moment later. "What is it?" he whispered.

"Shh," Quinn breathed, listening hard.

"After all, without their mapmakers, the problem of the Verdanians disappears like that." Forden snapped his fingers.

"Ah, master, we must be patient," said Morpeth. "After all, we have our own quest to complete – and you are not happy with our mapmaker at all. We have nothing to lose by waiting for the map – and everything to gain by taking that boy, Monstruo, with us if it proves to be better than ours."

Quinn frowned. What map?

"He is late."

"He will be here," Morpeth soothed.

"At least that infernal noise has stopped," Forden grumbled, his voice moving away again.

"Tell me what they said," Ajax whispered.

Quinn filled him in.

"I'm glad they went off the idea of killing us," said Ajax, grimly.

"I just wish we could get out of here," said Quinn. "I don't really want to stick around to see who's coming."

They had spent their time trying various methods of escape. Quinn had stood on Ajax's shoulders, but was too short to drag himself over the top of the pit. They had tried digging footholds into the earthen walls of their prison with Ajax's knife, but the loamy soil crumbled and Quinn was worried they'd bring a cascade of dirt down to suffocate them.

"Well, I'll just have to stick this into anyone who comes down to get us," Ajax had said, fingering his knife.

Now they could only wait, feeling helpless.

"I'd give anything for a mug full of rainwater right now," said Ajax.

"Don't talk about it," said Quinn, who had been trying to ignore his own raging thirst.

"We could ask them for a drink?"

"No!" hissed Quinn. "We don't want them coming over here – they'll see that there are only two of us."

Ajax sighed. "Did you ever imagine that we'd end up here? Seriously, in all that worrying you did about coming on this journey, did you ever think, 'Oh, we'll end up in a dirty pit, surrounded by Gelynions'?"

Quinn had to laugh. Ajax had been the only one at mapmaker school who had known just how much Quinn *didn't* want to be chosen for the honor of taking part in the King's quest. "No," he said, slowly. "Most of my 'worst-case' scenarios had to do with sailing off the edge of the world, into the waiting jaws of Genesi."

"I think that would be preferable," said Ajax. "Much better to die by fire-breathing dragon than like this."

Quinn was about to respond when his ears caught the sound of a new voice.

"At last!"

"That's Odilon!" said Ajax, jumping to his feet. "We're saved!"

"Shh," said Quinn, pulling him back down. "Listen."

"Shouldn't we shout and let him know we're here?" Ajax was confused.

"Wait," said Quinn, putting a hand on his friend's arm. "Remember the drawing? It sounds as though he's expected."

"About time," Morpeth was saying, in Suspite. "We had almost given up on you."

"Well, if you hadn't chosen such a ridiculous spot for the meeting, we'd have been here ages ago," said Odilon, querulously.

Quinn grimaced as he recognized that whining tone, which seemed to be Odilon's natural timbre.

"Did you particularly want your, er, friends to witness this?" asked Morpeth.

"It doesn't matter. We're here now and we want to be gone on the evening tide, so let's get this over with."

"You have what we need?"

"Yes, here." There was a sound of rustling, then a long pause.

"Ah, I see," said Forden, quietly, in Gelynion. "It is much more detailed than ours." Quinn assumed he was talking to Morpeth.

"So that's my end of the bargain," said Odilon. "I assume you've done your part."

There was another pause and fierce whispering. Quinn could only imagine that Morpeth and Forden were conferring.

"Yes," Morpeth said eventually. "I will get the boy."

The sound of heavy footsteps moved closer to the top of the pit.

"Quick," said Quinn. "Rub dirt on your face."

"What, more dirt?" said Ajax.

"Just do it," said Quinn, blackening his face further. He remembered that it was only the paleness of their faces that had shown him that there were three people in this pit. The longer it took the Gelynions to work out that Ira was gone, the better. It would give Ash more time to get help.

Morpeth loomed large overhead.

"It's very dark in there," he called to Forden in Gelynion.

"Never mind that, just get the redhead."

A rope was thrown down over the top. "Redhead, grab hold," said Morpeth in Suspite, peering down.

Quinn nudged Ajax. "They want you."

"I don't want to leave you here," whispered Ajax, urgently.

"You have to," said Quinn. "You're of much more use to me up there than you are down here. If you do nothing else, get a message to Zain."

"I'll try," said Ajax, clasping his friend's shoulder, before grabbing hold of the rope and pulling himself up, hand over hand, feet walking up the wall.

"What about the blond?" Morpeth called, as Ajax scrambled over the mouth of the pit.

"Leave him for now," said Forden.

Down in the pit, Quinn wished for one brief moment that Ira was indeed with him – even that would be better than being alone.

"Ah, Ajax," he heard Odilon say. "Good to see you. Let's go."

"But what about Quinn?" Ajax said, bewildered.

"Don't worry about him, Juan Forden will look after him."

"What have you done?" Ajax challenged.

"Nothing that need concern you, boy. I am your captain and you are a mere scribe. Now do as you're told and come with us. Or must I ask Jeremiah to convince you."

"I'm coming," said Ajax, uncertainly, "but you won't get away with this."

"Disagreeing with your captain is called mutiny," said Odilon, silkily. "And mutiny is punishable by death. The only reason that you are still alive is that I need to get the map finished. Don't think I haven't noticed your insubordination since you returned from the *Libertas*."

Quinn knew just how much Ajax had not wanted to go back to Odilon's ship, and he was beginning to see why.

"If you are quite finished," Morpeth interrupted. "We have what we need."

"Yes, you do," said Odilon.

"Just how did you come by this, by the way?" asked Morpeth.

"It was much easier than expected," said Odilon, happy to chat now that he had Ajax in sight. "Zain has picked up a Northern boy and he was most eager to help. I didn't even have to pay him. It seems he has his own reasons for wanting to be rid of the farm boy."

Kurt! What had he done? Quinn's fists clenched helplessly. He'd known Kurt wasn't to be trusted.

Morpeth sniggered. "Yes, we have also found Kurt to be most helpful. Well, it seems that we have all gotten what we wanted. Now, may the best man win."

"Indeed," said Odilon, making it clear that he thought he was the best man. "And that definitely won't be Zain. It's been a pleasure doing business with you."

"You should go that way back to your ship," said Morpeth, and Quinn wondered where he was pointing. "Much less possibility of running into anyone."

"Much obliged," said Odilon. "The fewer people who know where we've been, the better."

There were noisy sounds of departure and then the clearing was quiet once more.

"I wonder if the Verdanians know that their worst enemy is within their own ranks," said Forden.

"Well, not the worst," said Morpeth, laughing heartily. "But certainly the closest."

"Let us grab the dark-haired boy and be on our way," said Forden. "I want to be on that tide as well."

"And the blond one?"

"Kill him," said Forden, casually. "We have no need of him, and one less Verdanian mapmaker is no great loss."

Quinn shivered. It seemed that Ira's callousness had saved his life. Quinn's parents had always taught him that it was important to help others, but maybe, out here, he needed to think more about helping himself.

Now might be a good time to start.

Chapter Five

Zain was beginning to think that Tomas was taking them on a wild goose chase. He had led them out of the port and they were now bustling down a long, dirt road. A very dark road.

"Are you sure this is the way?" Zain queried, holding his burning torch a little higher.

"Yes," said Tomas. "There's a small outpost down this road. I left them there."

"What were they doing all the way out here?" Zain wondered.

"They went to the river."

"You're very well informed," said Zain, mildly.

"I, er, had to come this way," stammered Tomas.

Followed them, more like, thought Zain. Frey trotted along beside them, saying nothing. He had insisted on accompanying the Verdanians, "to help," though Zain knew it was more about keeping an eye on his son.

That was okay. He didn't trust Frey either.

"Is there only one road out here?" he asked.

"One main road," said Tomas. "There is a hunter's track over there but nobody uses that after dark. Too many dangers out in the trees."

Looking at the walls of green on either side of the road, Zain shivered. He was afraid of no man, but the idea of unknown creatures in an unknown land . . . well, that was something else.

"Yes. It's a harsh place," said Frey, noticing Zain's shudder. "Hot and wet all year round. If you turn your back for five minutes, the plants take over, growing into every crack and crevice."

"I can well imagine," said Zain, eyeing the predatory plant life. "And yet, here you are."

"Yes," said Frey, shortly.

As though on cue, a rumble of thunder sounded in the distance and Zain smelled the fresh, sharp scent of rain on the air. The clouds that were now keeping the moon from view would soon unleash their burden.

Zain was about to question Frey more closely when he heard a shout from Abel, who had rounded a bend ahead of the main group. He picked up his own pace, gesturing for the others to follow.

"Ash!" he exclaimed in relief, when Abel came into sight, holding his lit torch over the girl. "But where's Quinn?" The two were never far apart.

"Oh, Zain," Ash cried, and Zain noticed that she was shaking, despite the heat. "The Gelynions have him! They took me, thinking I was him, and then he came and got me out of the pit and told me to run, but I've left him there with Ira and Ajax and . . . the chattering creatures. Oh, Zain," she said again.

She was on the verge of tears, Zain could see, but holding it together. She was a tough little customer, this girl, he thought – no wonder none of his crew doubted the story that she was a boy.

But he had more important things to think of now.

"Quinn is with Ira and Ajax?" The garbled details about the pit were something he could ask more about later.

"Yes." Behind him, Dolan, who had been silent until now, exhaled sharply.

"And all three are with the Gelynions?" The question of why and how was also something to be addressed at a later date.

"Yes."

"Then why," said Zain, slowly, "is Ira following you down this road?"

Ash turned in alarm, all thoughts of tears gone. "Maybe Odilon rescued them!"

"Odilon?" said Zain, but Ash did not hear him.

"Ira!" she called out, running back to meet the blond boy, who was now walking towards them uncertainly. "You escaped! Where's Quinn?"

She looked down the road behind Ira. There was no sign of anyone else in the darkness.

Ira said nothing. Dolan pushed his way to the front of the pack.

"Ira?" said Ash, voice wavering a little.

The boy appeared to take heart from the sudden appearance of his captain.

"He's . . ." Ira paused. "He's dead. I'm sorry, but he's dead."

Zain's heart sank to his boots at the words, though he allowed his face to show nothing. He noticed the quick flash of satisfaction that crossed Dolan's face – and the uneasiness in Ira's.

"But, but . . . he can't be," said Ash. "He helped me escape. He was helping you escape. And you're here."

Yes, thought Zain, *Ira is here. And Quinn is not.*

"He, er, pulled me out of the pit and, er, told me to run – just like he told you," Ira said defensively, pointing at Ash. "And so I, er, ran into the trees and then I, er, heard noises and I looked behind and they, er, killed him."

Listening to the boy stammer through this recount of events, Zain couldn't help but think there was more to the story.

"And you could do nothing to help him?" he asked Ira, keeping his tone even.

"Of course not!" The boy's temper flared. "They would only have killed me too!"

"I'm sure that Ira did everything he could," said Dolan, moving to stand beside his mapmaker.

"Of course," said Zain. "And Ajax? What of him?"

"I don't know!" Ira shouted. "I didn't stick around to find out."

"You left him there? You just ran off and left him?" Ash was crying silently now, her tears glistening in the light of the torches. "What about Odilon? Did you see him?"

"Odilon?" Ira looked at her curiously. "No."

"Did you?" Zain interjected.

"I heard him in the dark," she said. "Somewhere in the trees. And there was the drawing . . ."

"Drawing?" Zain was struggling to follow the girl's story.

"Ajax's drawing of Odilon with Juan Forden," she snapped, before rushing on, allowing Zain no room for the many questions filling his head.

"So you just left Ajax?"

"What could I do?" whined Ira. "There were more of them than me."

"You could have tried *something*!" Ash's loathing for Ira was clear in every syllable.

"Yes, well, there was nothing I could do," repeated Ira, pulling himself up to stand straighter and looking down that haughty nose of his at Ash. "And I don't appreciate a *farm boy* like you questioning my actions."

Before Zain could stop her, Ash launched herself at Ira, throwing a very credible right hook in his direction, then used her momentum to sweep his legs out from under him with her left foot. Zain couldn't help but admire her technique for a moment – she'd obviously been working very hard at their morning training sessions – before he stepped in to break up the scuffle.

"Did you see that?" Ira moaned as he rubbed his jaw. "That stupid boy attacked me."

"I saw nothing," said Zain, before looking around at the rest of the group. "Did anyone here see anything?"

They all shook their heads.

"Bah!" said Dolan, "What more could I expect from a bunch of slaves and peasants and –" he looked Frey and Tomas up and down, "– whoever you are. Well, it won't matter now. Your mapmaker is gone and you have no reason to go on."

Ash growled at his words, and Zain put a hand on her shoulder to quiet her.

"Thank you for your words of sympathy," he said to Dolan. "I'm sure that you and Ira can find your own way back to the port."

"Wh-wh-where are you going?" asked Ira.

"To find Quinn," said Zain. "Even if he is dead, as you say, we will not leave him here. And to find Ajax, who may be in need of our help." *And to find Odilon and get some answers to my questions,* he added silently.

"Do what you want," said Dolan. "We will sail on the evening tide. Not that it matters to you. You are out of the race."

"We shall see," said Zain, quietly. "We shall see. Ash, can you find your way back to where you last saw Quinn?"

"I think so," she said.

Tomas stepped forward. "I think I know where it is," he said. "There's a hunter's stop a little farther on, and then through the trees. The *hombrecito* live there."

"Hombrecito?" whispered Ash.

"Those little creatures you heard," said Tomas. "Come."

As they moved on down the road, Zain felt a tug on his shirt. "Do you think he's really dead?" Ash whispered.

Zain paused. "You must prepare yourself that he may be," he said. "But . . ."

"Yes?" she said eagerly.

"I suspect that Morpeth and Forden would have more reasons for keeping Quinn alive than for killing him," said Zain, remembering their interest in his mapmaker up in the frozen village in the north.

"But why would Ira lie?"

"Quinn does not fit Ira's world view," said Zain, trying to explain it as simply as possible. "If Quinn is gone, there is no threat to Ira. Besides, much better to tell Quinn's friends that he is dead than to admit that you abandoned the boy who rescued you. Particularly to his friends."

"I hope you're right," Ash whispered fervently, squeezing his hand before releasing it.

So do I, Zain thought. "You must tell me more of Odilon," he went on. "What was he saying?"

"He was talking about maps," she said in a subdued voice. "No, about *copies* of a map . . . Oh, and I have this."

She pulled a piece of parchment from her pocket and Zain examined it by torchlight as they walked.

"Ah," he said eventually, not liking the look of Ajax's drawing at all. "I'm sure there is a good reason for –"

He stopped, unable to come up with a plausible reason on the spot, knowing that any reason for this meeting did not bode well for Quinn. But Ash did not need to have that confirmed.

"Besides," Zain continued, with an enthusiasm he did not feel, as he pocketed the parchment, "Ajax was with Quinn, you said. Odilon will not risk his mapmaker. All will be well."

"I hope you're right," Ash said again, looking unconvinced by his bluff, hearty tone.

Zain held his torch higher. "Of course," he said. "But we might just pick up the pace . . . just in case Odilon, er, needs a hand."

Quinn's situation was not getting any better. Gagged, wrapped in sacking from neck to toe, and with his hands and feet bound, he was slung around Morpeth's neck like the sides of pig his da slaughtered for the May festival. His head banged against the giant Deslonder's elbow at regular intervals and he was beginning to lose feeling in his feet.

"How much farther?" Morpeth grunted. "Even the slightest weight grows heavy over distances."

"Stop your bellyaching," Forden responded.

Quinn had never been so glad that he understood another language – and that this understanding was a secret. The Gelynions had been speaking freely in front of him ever since they'd found him in the pit by himself.

Despite initial consternation at Ira's escape, they were not worried enough to send a party to chase him down.

"The trees will do our work for us," said Forden. "He will die out here, lost and afraid."

Which would have been true, Quinn had thought, had Ira not listened to Quinn's own instructions to Ash on how to get back to the road. As it was, Quinn had remained calm, thinking that Ash, at least, would have made it back to port and even now would be on her way back with Zain to rescue him.

What he hadn't bargained on, however, was the speed with which the Gelynions had moved. Within minutes, they had doused the fire, trussed him up, and been off – down a winding trail that seemed to head in the opposite direction from the road.

Dazed and confused by his method of transport, Quinn found it difficult to orientate himself in the darkness. All he could hear was the trample of feet on the ground, each thud reverberating up through his body. Tree branches slapped at his face, and Morpeth kept hiking him up, obviously shifting Quinn's weight across his shoulders.

Thunder rumbled overhead and Quinn rolled his eyes, his only method of expression. All he needed now to add to his joy was a thunderstorm.

"Rain's coming," spat Morpeth.

"It is true what they say – you *are* a genius," said Forden, sarcastically.

Morpeth grunted.

"Less talk, more walk," continued Forden. "I want to catch that tide. It wouldn't do to be stranded in port with our . . . cargo."

"Indeed," said Morpeth.

After that, there was nothing except torches in the blackness and trees and the *thump-thump* of Morpeth's boots on the ground. Quinn drifted off, trying to find a place in his mind where the reality of being kidnapped would disappear. He flicked through his memory, conjuring up pictures of his brothers laughing and wrestling. Jed, so big and strong, so stifled by life on the farm. Simon, sneaking off with Merry, the blacksmith's daughter, whenever he thought no one was looking. Heath and Berrick, hardworking and amiable, each the other's best friend. And Allyn, only eighteen months older than Quinn, and ready to get him in trouble at every opportunity.

Even Allyn couldn't have come up with something like this.

He was jerked out of his thoughts by the realization that he was back on the streets around the port. They'd entered the town at a different point to the main road, and Quinn wondered how the Gelynions had known where to go.

He soon found out.

"Wait here," said Forden. "Cover his head."

Rough material was wrapped around Quinn's face. He could only be thankful that it was open weave, so he could breathe.

"Your hunting trip was successful?" asked a rough male voice in Suspite. Quinn didn't recognize it, but he tried to struggle against his bonds, to show the man that he wasn't a willing participant in this. Morpeth smacked the side of his head, and he subsided, dazed.

"Yes," said Forden, shortly, surprising Quinn. He had thought the man unable to speak Suspite, given that Morpeth had spoken for him with Odilon. "The hunter's trail led straight to the pit you suggested and it yielded results – well worth your payment."

"Excellent," said the man. "Why are you back then?"

"I had hoped you may have a strong, wooden cage."

"And why would you need one of those?"

"On a long journey such as ours, meat stays fresher if we keep it alive," said Forden.

"I see," said the man. "And if I had such a cage?"

"I would pay handsomely . . . of course," said Forden, and Quinn heard the clink of coins. "But it must be now. The evening tide won't wait."

"Very well then."

Quinn heard Forden's footsteps return. "Eso, Dra, you two bring the cage, quick as you can. We'll meet you on board."

With that, they were moving again as fat raindrops began to fall, Quinn's head thumping with every footstep. Worse than the pain, though, was the knowledge that he was about to board a Gelynion ship – followed closely by the cage that he suspected would be his accommodation.

Quinn groaned out loud in frustration, earning another elbow to the head from Morpeth. His only hope was that Ash and Zain were on his trail – but how would they even find the trail? If only he could drop something, anything, to let them know which way he'd gone. But his hands were tied and there was nothing he could do.

He could smell the sea now and knew that they must be close to the docks. Anger consumed him as he thought of Kurt on board the *Libertas*, in *his* cabin, safe and sound. Zain would never know what had happened, never know about the map that Kurt had given the Gelynions, never know about Odilon's treachery.

Would he even know that Quinn was alive? If he didn't, he wouldn't have a reason to chase the Gelynions!

Think, Quinn, think. He fought the black thoughts, trying to clear his mind, searching for a solution to his situation. The tight wrist bindings chafed his wrists and he wriggled his hands under him, trying to find a more comfortable position.

"Stop your wriggling," Morpeth hissed at him. "You're heavy enough as it is."

Quinn wriggled more. Anything to make the journey more difficult, anything to buy time. As he wriggled, he felt the bindings loosen, the soft cotton stretching with his efforts. He tried again.

"That's it!" said Morpeth, in frustration. Quinn felt a sickening lurch upward, and then he was dumped on the ground.

"Pick him up!" he heard Forden order.

"You pick him up," Morpeth answered. "You want him so badly, you carry him."

"May I remind you that you work for me." Forden's voice was calm, but Quinn could hear the cruel menace in it.

"How could I forget?" the Deslonder retorted. "But I am no beast of burden."

Quinn tuned out their argument, realizing that for the moment he'd been forgotten. Rocks poked into his back, and he wormed against them, feeling their sharp points pushing through the sacking in which he was wrapped as he continued to work at the bindings around his wrists. He would welcome a few bruises if he could just rip the sacking . . . He wished he could reach Ash's knife, still hidden down the side of his boot, but knew that pulling it out now, while bound and gagged, probably wasn't going to further his cause. Best to save that for a better moment.

Forden and Morpeth were still shouting at each other in Gelynion as he felt the fabric give beneath him. He shifted his hands and managed to get his right hand into his pocket, working it deep into the double-stitched seam.

And there it was. The large animal tooth that he'd found in the tribal village. The same one that had saved his life in Kurt's frozen hamlet. Quinn managed a grim smile. It was only fitting that he leave it here, hopefully to save him again, this time from Kurt's treachery.

He slid it from his pocket and, sweating with effort, shifted his body slightly to one side, using both hands to feel the sacking beneath him. The tooth caught in the fabric, and Quinn realized that it was a rip, tiny but . . . He pushed as hard as his bound hands would allow, and the point of the tooth went through the rip. Just a little more and . . .

"You two, pick him up," Forden said.

Quinn pushed harder, trying to ensure the tooth was through the sacking and under him before he was lifted again. Seconds later, he felt rough hands at his feet and shoulders, and then he was back in the air and being carried once again.

He wanted to scream and shout, but could do neither. All he could do was pin his hopes on a tooth, lying somewhere on a road, somewhere near the docks, in the dark, in an unknown land.

Which wasn't much as far as hopes went.

~

The clearing was empty, the fire at its center still smoking. Ash rushed to the far side, peering down into a large hole in the ground.

"This is where we were," she shouted.

"That's a trap," said Frey. "Hunters cover it with twigs and leaves and then hide behind the trees and wait for something to fall in."

"Is wildlife so plentiful here?" asked Zain.

"Yes," said Frey, simply. "We don't go hungry. But sometimes they get more than they bargain for, and find an angry serpent at the bottom . . ."

Zain grimaced.

"No sign of Quinn or Ajax," said Ash, returning to Zain's side. "No Odilon. Nobody."

"No," said Zain, looking around as the skies opened and the first raindrops fell. He was going to regret not fixing that hole in his boot. "But no sign of Quinn's body either."

"Is that good?" she asked, anxiously.

"I believe so. Forden would have no interest in taking it with him."

"Quinn's alive then?"

"The signs are good," said Zain.

The worried expression lifted from her face. "Well, let's find him then," she said.

"Yes," said Zain, "let's."

"They must have taken the hunting trail," said Frey. "Over there." He pointed to a narrow opening, barely discernible in the dark and the trees. The rain was coming harder now, and the soft ground around them was already turning to mud.

"Then so must we," said Zain.

The other Verdanians looked at each other.

"Do you think there will be serpents?" asked Ash.

"Possibly," said Frey.

"Oh," she breathed.

"If we make a lot of noise, they should avoid us," said Tomas.

Zain took note of the *should*.

"Right then," he said, looking at his wary crew. "We'll sing."

"Sing?" said Abel.

"Sing," confirmed Zain. "It should scare not only the serpents, but any Gelynions who may be nearby as well."

His words had the desired effect, as the group began arguing over exactly what should be sung, as they started towards the trail. Behind them, Zain silently picked up a large, heavy stick, and noticed that Frey did the same.

No sense in taking chances.

They moved swiftly through the trees in single file, brushing the rain from their faces and singing lustily, a selection of songs comprising some ribald sea shanties, an old Deslondic lullaby and a country ballad, sung by Dilly in a surprisingly tuneful voice. They had just taken up a spiritual hymn when Abel, at the front of the line, held up his hand, indicating they should stop.

"We're back in town," he called in a loud whisper.

Zain's heart sank. No sign of the Gelynions, which meant they were farther ahead than he'd hoped. "We must hurry down to the docks now," he said. "Run! If they sail on the tide, we won't catch them. Find Forden's ship."

He cursed the busyness of this port, which had allowed the large black boat to sail in unnoticed. He could only hope it had yet to sail out again.

The Verdanians took off as one, hurtling down the dirt road towards the docks. Zain winced as the rocks underfoot pierced the thinning sole of his boot. The huts around them were dark and shuttered. Anything could happen on these streets, he thought, and there would be no witnesses.

"Ouch!" He stopped as the point of a sharp rock dug into his foot.

"What is it? Are you hurt?" Cleaver rushed back to his side, and Zain managed a smile at his loyal first mate.

"No, not hurt," he said, bending down to remove the offending stone. "Just paying the price for inattention to detail."

He worked the rock free and was about to throw it to one side of the road when Cleaver stopped him.

"That's an unusual color," he noted.

Zain put the rock in the palm of his hand and held it up to his torch for closer examination.

"It's a –"

"Tooth!" said Cleaver. "Quinn's animal tooth! He's alive!"

Zain clenched his fist around the tooth. "Yes," he said, "he is. Or was to this point anyway."

"I'll tell the others," said Cleaver, running off.

Zain wiggled his toes in his boot as he limped off in pursuit, clutching the tooth in his hand. He was unsurprised to see Ash tearing back down the road towards him.

"Is it true?" she panted.

He held the tooth out, and she reached to take it.

"We must find him," she said, clutching it in her hand.

Zain nodded. "We will," he said. "We will." But he wasn't sure if it was Ash he was reassuring, or himself.

Chapter Six

Quinn yawned and stretched as best he could within the tight confines of his cage. Quite why the Gelynions felt they needed to put him in here was a mystery. It wasn't like he was going to be leaving their ship anytime soon.

He wasn't sure how long they'd been at sea – he knew it had been dark when they'd carried him aboard their ship, the *Black Hawk*, but the hold had no windows so he had no way of telling the time. He'd bucked and kicked as best he could as they'd bundled him into the cage, but all that had earned him was another clip around the ear from Morpeth. They'd untied him and then he'd been left alone, in the dark – hot, hungry and thirsty.

He'd dozed off at some point, but he had no idea how long he'd slept. Now he was stiff, sore as well as hot, hungry and thirsty, and more than a little scared, he admitted to himself.

The worst part of the whole situation was knowing he was alone. Having been surrounded by brothers his whole life, there had been few moments where he'd had only his own wits to rely on. His brothers had no qualms about teasing him or throwing a friendly punch in his direction, but woe betide any outsider who'd tried to poke fun at Quinn and his quiet ways.

Even aboard the *Libertas*, he'd had Ash. It had been for Quinn's sake that Zain had allowed Ash to stay aboard after she'd stowed away. He'd been horribly homesick, and Ash had been the tonic he'd needed.

But now . . .

Quinn shifted his weight, trying to alleviate the pressure of the cage's wooden slats underneath him. He really hoped that he wouldn't have to stay here, in the dark, for too long.

Then again, the alternative might be worse. He could feel the reassuring presence of Ash's knife in his boot, but wasn't entirely sure what good it would do him on a boat full of armed Gelynions.

As though his thoughts had conjured them up, he heard the tramp of boots overhead and then the clatter of the trapdoor to the hold opening.

Morpeth descended the rope ladder. "Ah, little mapmaker, you are awake," he said in Suspite, holding a lit torch over the cage.

Quinn winced as the light hit his eyes.

"Juan Forden wishes to meet with you." He untied the cage door and, grabbing Quinn by the ankle, dragged him through it. "Up you get," he said, gaily, almost as though they were playing a party game.

Quinn stood gingerly on shaky legs.

"In front of me," said Morpeth. "Up the ladder. Go on!" He gave Quinn a shove that nearly knocked him off his feet.

Quinn had no choice but to climb the rope ladder, feeling all of his muscles protesting as he went.

He emerged into the cabin area of the ship, and looked around with interest. Zain would want to know the details, and thinking about that would keep his mind focused.

The first thing he noticed was how dark it was. The passageway was narrow and lined with ebony wood. Three tiny open windows across the stern of the ship let in slivers of light, but even these were crisscrossed with fine latticework. Quinn wondered if the cabin portholes were any larger.

"That way," said Morpeth, interrupting his thoughts with another shove in the back. They walked down the passageway towards the bow.

"Stop," said Morpeth.

The passageway doglegged right and Quinn looked longingly up the stairs where he could see a patch of blue sky. It was morning then. He'd been aboard the ship at least one night.

"Move aside," said Morpeth, elbowing him out of the way to rap sharply on the large wooden door in front of them.

"Enter," Forden called out in Gelynion and Quinn nearly moved, remembering at the last second that he wasn't supposed to understand the language.

"In you go," said Morpeth, still speaking Suspite.

With a feeling of dread, Quinn walked through the door.

"About time," said Forden, in Gelynion, looking beyond Quinn to Morpeth. "You kept me waiting."

Quinn kept his face blank, though his eyes were busy taking in every detail of the big, luxurious cabin, which was certainly Forden's own. He was seated in front of them at a solid, ornate wooden desk. His oversized bed, built into the right-hand wall of the room, was topped with an over-stuffed mattress covered in a velvet comforter of deep burgundy and gold, and piled high with pillows. Here, the two portholes were large, though still with latticework. It might look decorative, Quinn thought, but it also acted as a barrier for prying eyes – or flying weapons.

His boots sank into the soft rugs beneath his feet, and he noticed that Forden had a carafe on his desk made from what looked like green glass. He stared. He hadn't seen glass outside of the King's palace, and then only for use by the royal family themselves.

"We are here now," said Morpeth. "Our little mouse here was just waking in his cage."

"Mouse, indeed," said Forden. "Monstruo Mouse."

Quinn only just kept himself from wincing at the use of the word. He hated being referred to as a freak, in any language.

"Tell him we will not harm him if he does what we say," said Forden.

Morpeth turned to Quinn, repeating Forden's words, translated into Suspite. Quinn took mental note of the fact that the great explorer chose not to reveal his fluency in the common language.

He nodded briefly.

"I have your map," Forden continued, with Morpeth translating in an undertone.

Quinn faked surprise, hiding his anger.

"My map?" he said, in Suspite.

Forden took a rolled parchment from his drawer and spread it over his desk. He beckoned Quinn closer.

Quinn edged in far enough to see that the parchment was, in fact, the fake map that he'd left in his cabin – confirming Kurt's role in all this.

Forden was grinning up at him as though he'd pulled off the best joke ever. Quinn had an overwhelming urge to reach over and pull hard on the man's ridiculous moustache, but he pushed it down. He would have his revenge on these men, when the time was right. If the nature of that revenge wasn't clear at this point, well, that didn't matter.

"Where did you get this?" he asked.

Morpeth laughed. "Sometimes it doesn't pay to take in strays – and it certainly never pays to trust your competitors," he said with a sneer. "The honorable Odilon told us all about you and your, er, talents. We had decided to simply take all three mapmakers at the first opportunity, giving your captains no reason to progress with their journeys. But then Odilon came to us with a proposition . . ."

Quinn said nothing, waiting for him to go on. Forden was sitting back in his chair with that smug grin on his face.

"Well," said Morpeth, when he realized he would get no reaction from Quinn. "He offered us your map. It seems that your friend Ajax had told him of its wonders. Odilon wanted to be the only Verdanian with a mapmaker . . . We decided it was of no consequence if he took the redhead – we would simply kill him the next time we saw him. Which we will."

Quinn gulped. He hoped that Odilon and Ajax didn't run into the Gelynions any time soon.

Morpeth saw the movement, and his cruel smile returned. "Don't like the sound of that, do you – I find it interesting that you worry for your friend's skin and do not seem to realize that your own is in more peril."

Quinn stared at the wall, trying not to look worried.

"Anyway, where was I? Oh yes. I don't know exactly how the *noble* Odilon planned to steal your map, but as it turned out, he didn't have to. Your *friend* Kurt handed it over without so much as blinking. It seems that he does not like you very much."

The feeling's mutual, thought Quinn, feeling his body tense all over as his anger at Kurt took hold.

"Odilon seemed to think that Kurt has designs on taking over your role as mapmaker," Morpeth mused. "He has kept a copy of your map and . . . Well, he is a survivor, as I recall . . . very adept at finding a place for himself."

Quinn knew that Morpeth was referring to the help Kurt had given the Gelynions, even after they'd killed everyone in Kurt's village, including his parents.

"So, little mapmaker," said Forden, clearly deciding that Morpeth's monologue in Suspite had gone on long enough. "Now you are with us, and your map is with us."

As Morpeth translated, Quinn studied Forden's face. His eyes were a murky brown, deep set above his hooked nose. Black eyebrows beetled their way over his forehead, and his dark, curly hair was tied at the nape of his neck. Ajax's drawing of him had really been rather good, Quinn decided.

". . . you understand?" Quinn realized that Forden was still speaking, and that he'd missed most of what had been said. Thankfully, Morpeth's voice droned in his ear, translating.

"You will continue to make your map," he said. "And, if you want to stay alive, you will do a good job . . . or else." Quinn knew that Morpeth had added the last words himself and, judging by his leering grin, enjoyed them.

"I . . ." Quinn began. There was so much he wanted to say, beginning with telling Forden where to stick his map and his ridiculous moustache. But he could hear Zain's voice in his mind: "You cannot change what other people will do. You can only change how you react to those things."

He couldn't change the situation right now. All he could do was to make the best of it and wait until the time was right.

Zain would come for him.

He *had* to come.

Either that, or Quinn's swimming skills were going to be tested.

To Forden, he nodded.

"Excellent," said the Gelynion. "I knew you'd see it my way." He clapped his hands twice.

The door opened and a shabby, balding man entered. He was quivering from head to foot, and grinding his teeth.

"Yes, Count Forden," he said, bowing to the explorer. "You wanted me?"

"Yergon," said Forden, drawing the name out like a curse. "You are no longer needed."

The man's mouth dropped open. "What? Why?"

"I have a new mapmaker," Forden replied. "You have made too many mistakes."

"B-b-but . . ." the man stammered.

Quinn shifted uncomfortably. He was not supposed to be able to understand what was being said, but Yergon's sheer terror unnerved him.

Forden sighed. "How am I to map the world and win the further admiration of the Queen when I am surrounded by idiots? Simple answer: I am not. And so you are relieved of your duties. Look at this map!"

He held it up for inspection and Yergon crept closer to view it. "You see the detail, you see the precise line work, the illustration – the color? *This* is what I need to finally prove to Rey Bernadino that I am the greatest explorer Gelyn has ever seen – and *he* will do it for me."

All eyes in the room followed Forden's finger, pointing directly at Quinn, who tried to look as though he had no idea of what was being said.

"It is indeed beautiful, sire," said Yergon, studying it closely. "Though I wonder how you know that it is accurate." He raised his eyes to look at Quinn.

This man is not stupid, thought Quinn, seeing the questions in Yergon's eyes. It seemed he had noticed the inconsistencies in the map.

"I know things about this boy that confirm it," was all Forden said. "And I do not need to explain it to you."

"And what of me?" Yergon asked, still looking at Quinn.

"You," said Forden, with a smile. "You get whipped and then you walk the plank. I have no need of a useless mouth to feed."

Quinn's involuntary "No!" was fortunately covered by Yergon's dramatic scream.

"No, master, no," he wailed, dropping to his knees on the soft rug. "I can do better, I can –"

"Enough!" Forden clapped his hands again. "Morpeth!"

"Yes, sire."

"Whip this man. Just enough to scream, not enough to bleed. I want him conscious when he walks the plank. He is proud of being the only man on the *Black Hawk* who can swim – let us see him do it."

"It shall be done." Morpeth grabbed Yergon by the back of his dirty, white shirt.

"Er." Quinn had spoken without thought.

"Yes," said Morpeth, as Forden's eyes swung towards him.

"What's, er, happening?" Quinn asked in Suspite, feigning innocence.

"Nothing for you to be concerned about." Morpeth spoke in a low voice.

"Who's he?" Quinn pointed at Yergon, who had gone limp in Morpeth's grip.

"Your predecessor," said Morpeth, shortly. "Take heed. Forden does not suffer shoddy workmanship."

"What's going to happen to him?"

"Why the delay?" asked Forden, impatiently.

"Monstruo Mouse asks many questions," said Morpeth.

"Only . . ." said Quinn, desperately. His mind was racing. He had no desire to be the cause of another man's death – and he had every reason for trying to find himself an ally on this wretched ship. "I could use some help."

"Help?" said Morpeth, raising one eyebrow in a way that reminded Quinn momentarily of Zain. Quinn wondered if that particular trick was one learned by every boy in Deslond.

"Yes, er, you know, to mix colors and do calculations . . ."

"We were under the impression that you worked alone," said Morpeth, looming over him. Yergon had stopped twitching and was now watching the proceedings with great interest.

Quinn wondered how much Suspite he understood. "Well, yes, I do," said Quinn, knowing he shouldn't overplay his hand. "But there was always someone around to assist. The map is the key to everything, after all . . ." He had a sudden burst of inspiration. "Zain understood that."

Morpeth reacted as Quinn had hoped he would. "Zain!" he spat. "What would he know?" It was clear he would not allow himself to be outdone by Zain on any level.

Morpeth turned to Forden. "I think you should keep this wretch," he said, as though the whole thing was his idea. "The boy could use some help to create the map. After all, the map is the key to everything."

Quinn suppressed a victorious smile as Forden considered it. Yergon didn't move a muscle.

"All right then," Forden said. "For now, take them both to the hold."

Quinn stopped smiling.

"You can keep him, Monstruo Mouse," said Morpeth, laughing. "I'm sure you'll be very cozy in your cage together."

Quinn took a deep breath. "About that," he began. "It's very hard to work on a map in the dark. Surely you have somewhere more suitable for me?"

Morpeth laughed again. "Don't push it, little mouse," he said. "We have some space set aside for you near the wheelhouse, under the watchful eye of the first mate. When you're not there, working, you'll go back to your comfortable little cage. With your new friend."

Quinn sighed as he followed Morpeth from the cabin. He knew he'd done the right thing for Yergon in saving him from certain death. Whether it was the right thing for himself, however, remained to be seen.

"So, I was thinking, I could take over the mapmaking duties."

Zain looked down at the boy before him, taking in Kurt's sharp features and obsequious expression. Was it his imagination or did the Northern boy seem more relaxed now that Quinn was gone? "Take over? That seems to suggest that you don't believe we will find Quinn."

"I, er, no, of course we will find him," said Kurt, no longer meeting Zain's eyes. "But, you know, until he returns."

Thinking of Quinn's horror if he allowed Kurt anywhere near his precious map, Zain shook his head. "For now, there is no need," he said. "If too much time and distance passes, we shall see."

Kurt's expression, which had fallen at his first words, brightened once again.

You don't think he's coming back, Zain thought, watching Kurt closely. He had paid no particular attention to Quinn's dislike of this boy, putting it down simply to having to share his space. But now he wondered.

Then again, they were currently on a wild-goose chase, looking for Quinn on a Gelynion ship, all based on finding a tooth . . . so maybe Kurt wasn't so wrong to be doubtful.

Zain stared out at the endless ocean. He was aware of Kurt slinking out of the wheelhouse, but his mind was elsewhere.

The *Libertas* had set sail before the sun's rays slid over the horizon. Even so, Zain knew they were a good twelve hours behind the Gelynions. Sailing out of the harbor, leaving the still-sleeping port in their wake, Zain had taken the decision to continue sailing south.

"They won't retrace old ground," he said to Cleaver. "They don't know that we're on the trail, so they'll push forward."

Cleaver had nodded. He was a gruff, no-nonsense man, but Zain knew he'd developed a soft spot for Quinn. He'd broached the subject of Quinn's unusual memory only once, as the two men were enjoying a rare, peaceful moment in the wheelhouse one day.

"He's a smart 'un," Cleaver had said.

"That he is," conceded Zain.

There'd been a pause.

"Some might think there were some magic in him," Cleaver continued.

Zain chose his words carefully, knowing that the crew would follow Cleaver's lead in their treatment of Quinn.

"Not magic," he said. "A gift."

Cleaver had nodded slowly. A gift was something good, something bestowed. Whereas magic was something that could go either way.

"A gift," he'd agreed, and Zain had breathed a sigh of relief. Life on board a ship was difficult enough without having to protect his mapmaker from a suspicious, hostile crew.

Speaking of gifts, Zain's thoughts turned to the gems locked away in one of the secret compartments in his cabin. A glittering pile of precious stones, most of them dark, burnished yellow.

Nobody had been more astonished than he when Frey had turned up at the docks that morning, Tomas in tow, carrying a sack.

"I want you to take him," Frey had said, pushing his son forward. The boy was wearing a strange facsimile of Verdanian clothing – lightweight cotton breeches, and a flowing shirt in the Verdanian style, but in bright-red fabric.

Zain blinked.

"I . . . have no need of him."

"In exchange for information," said Frey, "about that boy of yours."

Zain hesitated. "I'm listening," he said. "But make it quick."

Frey had nodded, and explained that he'd asked around the port after the Verdanians had returned to the *Libertas*. He'd found a man who'd admitted to giving hunting tips to some foreigners the day before. They'd returned that night, Frey said, with their prey, wrapped in sackcloth, carried by what had been described as a huge bull of a man.

"Wrapped?" Zain asked quickly. "Alive or dead?"

"Alive," Frey confirmed. "They bought a cage – to keep their catch 'fresh.'"

Zain shuddered at the image. "I see," he said. "But I still see no reason to take your boy."

Frey stared at him, sizing him up. "Very well, then," he said. "I will pay for his passage with these." He opened the sack and pulled out a roll of the vibrant wall hangings that Zain had last seen in his home.

"What would I do with these?" he asked, taken aback. What man would send his son off with strangers, probably never to be seen again?

"Look at them," said Frey, roughly. "Look closely."

Zain had picked up the top rug, which sparkled under the watch light as the beads caught the glow. "It is a fine piece of work," he said, holding it loosely. "But –"

"Look closely," repeated Frey, and Zain did, taking only seconds to realize what he was seeing.

"These are not beads," he said.

"No," said Frey. "We both know what they are."

Frey was not going to say it, Zain realized. He would not admit his guilt aloud.

"You are giving them back," Zain said.

"In return for safe passage for Tomas," said Frey.

"Why would you send away your only son?"

"I want him to know Verdania," said Frey. "I want him to see the twilight and the cobbled streets and the green fields. I want him to have what I no longer have."

"And his mother? She agrees with this?" Zain's gaze turned to Tomas, whose eyes were red rimmed.

"She does," was all Frey said, and Zain could hear the echo of hours of argument in those two words.

"I am surprised you still have these," said Zain, flicking through the rugs. "You could have sold them and lived like a king."

Frey laughed, the sound harsh in the morning air. "You'd think!" he said. "But they're worthless. Outside of Verdania, they're worthless!"

"Worthless?" repeated Zain, astounded.

"Here, if it's not gold, it's not worth anything," said Frey. "And they have so much gold it's practically worthless anyway. That's why I've included a bag of gold dust here. I showed them those loganstones and they laughed at me. Told me I should use them as beads."

And so you did, thought Zain, holding King Orel's most precious treasure in his hands.

"You might as well take them back," said Frey. "I have no use for them. They've been nothing but trouble. Just make sure that Tomas gets a few of the other stones, you know, to get started when he gets there."

There was a pause.

"So will you?" Frey pressed. "Take him, that is."

"Only if he wants to go," Zain said. "Unlike others, I am not in the business of forcing children onto ships when they do not wish to go."

Tomas had nodded, hesitantly. "I would," he said. "I am almost a man. Soon there will be no place for me in my father's home anyway."

At that, father and son had embraced fiercely, and Frey had handed Zain a crumbling piece of parchment. "This might be useful," he said.

Opening it, Zain saw that it was a roughly drawn map of the coast. "We are on a peninsula," Zain said, noting that the coastline continued only a little farther south, before turning back on itself. A small island was drawn on the other side of the headland. "What is this?" he asked, pointing to it.

"That's where Keila's father found me," said Frey. "I drifted for days and days, clinging to a piece of driftwood and washed up on that island. Weeks later, Keila's father's boat appeared on the horizon and I managed to build a big enough fire to attract their attention."

"I see," said Zain. "And how did you manage to dissuade them from killing you?"

Frey looked at his feet. "That's what I was just about to tell you." He looked up at Zain. "They're pirates," he admitted. "One boat in hundreds that swarm around this headland and into those waters." He indicated the vast stretch of ocean on the other side.

"I gave them the gold I had, and showed them the stones." He laughed bitterly. "They threw the stones back at me, but kept the gold."

"And you've earned your living by sailing with them ever since," surmised Zain.

"Yes," said Frey. "Now do you see why I want Tomas out of here? It's no life for anyone."

Zain nodded. "I will take care of him."

Frey looked away. "I saw you search for your mapmaker. That's why I chose you. I know you will."

And with that, it was done. Frey embraced his son once more and went back down the gangplank without a backward glance, leaving Tomas standing silently before the now-gathered *Libertas* crew.

"Well," said Zain, watching Tomas watch his father leave. "It seems we have a new crew member. You have sailed with your father?"

The boy nodded.

"Stow your belongings in Quinn's cabin for now," said Zain, motioning Kurt forward. "Kurt will show you. Then report back here. We will see exactly what you can do."

Now, as the sun finished its daily arc across the sky, Tomas was perched high above the deck, taking Quinn's turn at watch, despite Ash's protests. She had been up there most of the day, and would have stayed there all night had Zain allowed it. As it was, she was hanging over the rail at the bow of the *Libertas*, still watching.

Unlike Ash, Zain had no qualms about trusting the watch to Tomas. He had thrown himself into work that day, under Cleaver's watchful eye, and the first mate had had nothing but praise for the boy's skills.

"'E's been trained well," Cleaver told Zain.

As a pirate would be, Zain had thought. But he sensed a desperation in the boy as well – he was trying to keep himself busy so as not to think about what he was leaving behind. Zain could understand that.

"Watch report," he called out now.

"All clear," came the shout from the crow's nest. "Nothing to report."

On a normal day, the all clear was what any captain wanted to hear. But today Zain would have given anything to hear Tomas shout, "Sail ho!"

"Where are you, Quinn Freeman?" he muttered to himself. "Where are you?"

Chapter Seven

Quinn used his fingernail to scratch another mark in the frame of his cage. *Four*. He'd made the first one when he'd been returned to the hold by Morpeth on that first day, squeezing back into his accommodation with Yergon, who clearly was not a fan of soap and water. Since then, the pair had been up on deck three times, blinking in the sunlight and, in Quinn's case, gulping in fresh air while he could.

Tied together, they sat outside the wheelhouse, under the nose of whomever was steering the ship. This was usually an older man, streaks of gray through not only his hair but his moustache, who watched them silently and without interest – although he was quick to slap Quinn over the back of the head if he caught him staring around the deck. He was probably the first mate, Quinn had decided, trying to keep his head down even as he drank in as many details of Gelynion shipboard life as he could.

He'd noticed a large cage, similar to his own, behind the wheelhouse. It appeared to house upward of a dozen white seabirds, who sat, heads under wings, most of the time that Quinn was on deck. The only time they showed any life was when a crew member approached the cage with a bucket of fish, teasing the birds by dangling them through the top bars. Then, the squawking racket they made had Quinn covering his ears, even as he wondered what the birds were for. Did the Gelynions eat them?

Perhaps he'd ask Yergon – who probably wouldn't answer him. He spoke little. Quinn had tried to ask Yergon questions in Suspite, but he either had scant understanding of the common language or, like his captain, pretended not to. Quinn wasn't ready to reveal his knowledge of Gelynion, and so the two sat in silence, in the dark, most of the day.

On day three, when Quinn's fingers, cramped and useless from being squashed beside Yergon all night, had been unable to hold his quill, Forden had ordered that Morpeth find alternate lodgings for the Gelynion scribe, so he was now tied up each night to a stout post at the other end of the hold. Morpeth had thrown a thin blanket at Yergon and then, after a pause, dropped one through the bars of Quinn's cage as well. So now Quinn at least had a thin barrier between his body and the bottom bars of the cage.

Quinn had never been so grateful for his memory. He used it to conjure up a picture of his map – his real map – and, in his mind, added to it the details that he was observing during those brief, precious moments on deck. While he was up there he was, of course, working on the fake map, taking notes, making calculations, while Yergon looked on. Quinn hadn't yet tested his companion and was sticking to the true details of what he saw, but he had decided to insert some misleading calculations the following day, just to see what Yergon did.

If he reported Quinn's actions to Morpeth, well, one miscalculation could be easily explained as an error . . . But if he did not . . .

Quinn rolled over onto his back, ignoring the pressure from the wooden slats below him, and stared up into the blackness. So far, he had been a model prisoner, doing exactly what the Gelynions asked of him, biding his time. But as each day slipped away, he had begun to wonder what he was biding his time for. There was no opportunity for escape here. There was only the endless water and a group of short-tempered Gelynions, who shoved and jostled him every chance they got. Morpeth had taken pleasure in letting Quinn know that the crew didn't like having him on board.

"They think it would be better to kill you," he'd said. "They do not like the fact that you have put Yergon here out of a job."

Added to that was the fact that Forden kept them on short rations and his relentless need for speed meant that none of the crew was getting much rest. The *Black Hawk* simply went on and on under full sail, day and night.

Quinn wondered if the *Libertas* was doing the same, and felt a familiar surge of helplessness. He had no idea if Zain even knew that the Gelynions had him. He could only hope that Ash had been able to find her way back to the clearing and then . . .

And then, he thought, slapping his hand on the roof of the cage in frustration, they would have had to find the tooth, deduce that Forden had taken him – not killed him – and work out which way the Gelynions had gone, on a vast and featureless ocean, where everyone was making up their route as they went.

Quinn could feel himself sliding into lethargic despair and tried desperately to rouse himself. The combination of darkness and boredom was beginning to play on his mind, and he knew he had to fight it.

He conjured up a picture of his family in his mind, remembering a bright, hot summer's day in Markham the previous year. His father had been in a rare good mood, and given all the boys the day off, "just because," as he'd told their mother. They hadn't waited around for him to change his mind, but had run directly to the river, wrestling and laughing the whole way.

When they'd gotten there, they'd removed their shoes and waded in, enjoying the cool suck of the mud beneath their feet, watching the fish jump in the river, beyond their reach. Quinn had been so distracted by the splash and play of their silvery scales in the sunlight that he'd failed to notice Allyn creeping up behind him – until a firm shove in the middle of the back had sent him face-first into the water.

Flailing, eyes and nose full of water, Quinn had been struggling to find his feet when Allyn pushed him from behind again, roaring with laughter. Down Quinn went once more, gasping for breath, feet sliding out from under him.

"Oi!" said Jed, wading towards them. "He's had enough."

Allyn had laughed. "He'll have had enough when he shows me he won't take any more," he'd said, and Jed had laughed, too.

So delighted were the pair of them with Allyn's comic brilliance that they didn't notice that Quinn had regained his feet – enough to allow him to thrust his entire body at his brother's legs, grabbing Allyn around the knees and tackling him into the water. As Allyn fell, he clutched at Jed, dragging him down into the river with them, where all three rolled over and over in the muddy water.

"Oh," said Allyn, coming up for air, "I reckon he's had enough, Jed."

Lying in the dark now, Quinn allowed himself a small smile, even as his fists clenched. He'd had enough, he decided. Tomorrow, he would begin to fight his captors. He may not be able to save himself right now, but he would do what he could to undermine the Gelynion's efforts to map the world.

Even if no one in Verdania ever knew what he'd done.

Up on deck the next morning, Quinn removed his boots, as he always did, wriggling his toes in the sunshine. He was glad that Ash was not there to smell his socks – he would never live it down. With a small smile, he tucked them up into the open window of the wheelhouse above him. Quinn hoped that Streaky, as he'd nicknamed the first mate, enjoyed the aroma . . .

Ash's knife he'd left in the cage, rolled up neatly in his thin blanket, as he'd done every morning. And every night, he tucked it back into his sock before he tried to sleep, keeping it close in the dark, using it to keep inquisitive rats at bay.

A stiff breeze ruffled his hair and he sighed as he looked down at his map, which was getting grubby around the edges. He longed for his cozy cabin with its neat desk and lack of disruptive wind. He even missed his cloak – mostly it was warm enough to sit on deck in shirtsleeves, but on days like today an extra layer would be handy. He cursed the humidity that had caused him to leave it in his cabin that day he'd gone exploring with Ash and Ajax. Things changed so quickly in his world now.

Yergon nudged him, and he looked up quickly to see Morpeth striding towards them.

"Monstruo Mouse," said Morpeth. "How are you on this fine morning? I trust you slept well." He gave Quinn an evil grin.

"Like a baby," answered Quinn, plastering on an innocent smile. His mam, he remembered, had always claimed that babies never slept, so the expression fit well here.

"Excellent," said Morpeth, clapping his hands. "I have your charts for you." He held out two pieces of vellum, and Quinn took them. On one, Morpeth had marked the positions of the stars the previous night. On the other were someone's – Streaky's? – calculations of the ship's speed and direction.

"Juan Forden would like to inspect your mapping efforts this morning," Morpeth continued. "I will return in two bells to take you to him."

Watching Morpeth walk away, Quinn found his resolve wavering, wondering if today was a good day to begin his quiet rebellion. If Forden was going to examine his map closely, perhaps it would be better to wait until the next day . . .

Yergon shifted beside him, handing him his quill. The man's main role that morning would be to ensure that Quinn's tools did not blow away or roll down the deck.

The movement was enough to break Quinn's doubting thoughts. There was never a good time to start a fight. Even a quiet one. There was only now.

He took the quill from Yergon's hand, dipped it unsteadily into the ink pot the Gelynion held out, and began.

Checking the notes that he'd taken the day before, Quinn stared up at the sun, looking for minuscule changes in position. Next, he studied Morpeth's charts, noting as he did that the great north star was still absent. Which meant they were still nowhere near home.

Quinn stood up and scanned the horizon, looking for any sign of landfall to mark on his map. He saw nothing but white-capped waves, rolling and slapping against each other, and sat down quickly when he sensed Streaky moving to cuff him. The movement of the ocean intrigued Quinn. In his experience, waves tended to flow in one direction, but here, two sets appeared to be running headlong at each other, which might explain why the ship was rolling and bucking so much today when there was so sign of storm clouds in the sky. Quinn made a mental note to keep an eye on this phenomenon.

Yergon was watching him expectantly, and Quinn realized the quill was still in his hand. It was time to put his plan into action. He pulled out a fresh sheet of vellum. If there was one thing the Gelynions had a good supply of, it was this.

He began writing down his calculations, transferring Morpeth's charts and his own to the notes, aware of Yergon over his shoulder. At first he stayed true to the information he'd been given, but then, taking a deep breath, he casually moved a star. Then a second. Yergon stilled beside him.

Quinn said nothing and kept on transferring the information, this time changing three figures in Streaky's speed estimations. There was no protest from Yergon, though Quinn did hear him inhale sharply.

He felt a hand on his shoulder, and looked across into Yergon's clear brown eyes, trying to keep his expression innocent. This was an important moment. Would Yergon use Quinn's deception to try to win back favor with Forden? Or was he so sick of being treated badly, and so grateful to Quinn for saving his life, that he would say nothing?

The ship rocked and plunged beneath them as time stood still.

Yergon nodded. And Quinn breathed again.

He continued working steadily for several minutes, as the seabirds began a raucous squawking and cawing. Sticking his head around the corner of the wheelhouse, Quinn noticed they were jumping and flapping in their cage, distressed by the movement of the deck beneath them.

Scanning the deck, he thought that the same could be said of the Gelynion crew, who were running from one side of the ship to the other, peering over the sides.

"What's going on?" Quinn muttered, under his breath.

Beside him, Yergon drew his knees up to his chest and began chanting quietly in Gelynion. Quinn couldn't make out every word, but it seemed that his fellow mapmaker was praying to someone, anyone, to save them.

Suddenly the bow of the ship plunged downward, and Quinn was, for the first time since he'd been captured, happy that he was tied to the wheelhouse – without the tether he'd have slid all the way down the deck. As it was, Quinn collected a fine bunch of splinters in the seat of his breeches before he reached the end of the chain. He clutched his charts and his map in one hand and held on to the tether for dear life with the other.

Beside him, he could hear Yergon screaming in Gelynion, still chanting his prayer, the ink pot nowhere to be seen.

Just as suddenly, the bow jerked skyward, the long, pointed prow piercing the sky. Turning his head slightly, Quinn had a glimpse of the carved wooden woman on the front of the ship as she was thrust upward into the bright blue, her frozen, openmouthed features mirroring the expression of every man on board.

Taking advantage of the movement, Quinn scrabbled back along the deck and grabbed hold of the ring secured in the wood. Pushing his back against the wheelhouse wall, he tucked his charts and map down the front of his shirt and crouched. He'd had enough experience with wild weather now to know that it was much easier to balance on a ship when you were on your feet, allowing your weight to shift and change with the movement of the deck. In his early days on board the *Libertas*, before he'd "grown" his sea legs and when every movement of the ship had made him nauseous, his instinct had been to lie down – which hadn't helped one little bit.

"Come on," he said now to Yergon, who was sitting beside him, moaning. "Get up." He pulled on the man's shoulder and pointed to himself, indicating what Yergon needed to do. The man shook his head.

"Suit yourself," said Quinn, who had detected a pause in the upward motion of the ship. He braced for what seemed inevitable . . .

Sure enough, the *Black Hawk* plunged back downward with a crash, hitting the trough of the wave with enough force to throw Quinn's head back against the wheelhouse wall with a crack. Dazed, he shifted his feet, struggling to stay upright, as the sea spray doused him; Yergon had no chance, sliding back down the wood slats for another splintery ride.

Behind him, Quinn could hear Squeaky cursing and praying as he fought to hold the wheel steady. The deck was now slick with seawater and the Gelynions were holding tight to anything that seemed solid in a world that had gone crazy. Above them, in the still bright-blue sky, the sun shone benevolently.

Quinn shook his head. There was no explanation for these wild waves. There was a breeze, yes, but there was no storm, no gale-force winds – there was not even a sign of Nammu, the great white beast that had stuck with the *Libertas* on the first part of the journey. She had reared up out of the ocean, a huge head with a small eye, and what Ash had called a "fountain" of spray.

He had not seen Nammu since the sea had gone from navy to green and the temperatures from cold to humid. He missed the creature, which he had named, and which he thought of as "she." Quinn had always believed she'd brought them good luck and his feelings on that were only reinforced by the string of bad luck that had dogged his footsteps since he'd last sighted her.

Another shower of water brought him back to the present. Yergon had managed to drag himself up the deck and was now back beside Quinn, this time crouched on his feet, weight shifting with the movement of the deck.

"We're going to die!" he muttered in Suspite. Quinn turned to look at him in astonishment, and Yergon shrugged slightly. "I wasn't sure if I wanted to talk to you," he said in explanation, only just audible over the roar of the ocean.

"I saved your life," said Quinn, indignantly.

"True," said Yergon, grunting as he tried to keep his balance, "and I do thank you for that, but you must understand that this is a very difficult environment. Everyone is looking sideways at everyone else, and people will use any advantage to get in with Forden. I had to be sure."

Quinn shook his head in amazement. Wasn't it hard enough to be sailing into the unknown without taking dissent and backstabbing with you?

"What did I do to convince you I was worth talking to?" he asked. "If saving your life didn't do it, I can't imagine what would."

"You know," said Yergon, indicating the charts and map still stuffed inside Quinn's tunic.

Quinn nodded. "I'm not sure it's going to do us any good," he said. "Maps are quite useless at the bottom of the ocean."

Yergon paled. "I –" He stared at his feet.

Quinn turned to see what had made his new friend stop speaking so abruptly.

Morpeth loomed out of the sea spray, staggering and lurching with the movement of the ship. "Dinoh!" he shouted. "Dinoh!"

Streaky's head popped out of the wheelhouse. "What?" he spat.

"Steer to port!" ordered Morpeth. "There is calmer water that way."

Odd, thought Quinn. He stood up, craning his neck to see over the bulwark and railing, trying to get an idea of what was going on. The waves continued to rush at each other in a swirl of white water. It reminded him of the time that two of his father's bulls had taken umbrage with each other, blindly running into a clash of horns, bellowing and snorting. Two opposing forces going nowhere, fast.

As the ship creaked its way around to port, the sails flapping in protest, the bucking deck began to calm, and Quinn was able to pull out his map. He traced the northern coastline, superimposing the correct details over the fake ones in front of him. He thought about the color of the ocean up there. Thinking hard, he stood up for another look at the water around him.

With the ship changing direction he could see it. Beyond the boiling white water through which they currently sailed, the ocean's color deepened towards navy. If he turned his head the other way, it lightened towards green.

The meeting point between two oceans.

By his estimation, looking at the sun and the behavior of the sea, they were now sailing northeast. Back towards Verdania. Back towards home.

Except that Quinn wouldn't be going home.

Quinn was headed for Gelyn.

Chapter Eight

Ten. As Ash lined up for morning training, all she could think was that Quinn was not there again. For the tenth time since they'd left Barbarin. Tomas, standing beside her, copying her every move, gave her an encouraging smile, but Ash couldn't return it. Her mood was as gray as the skies above her.

It was their third day of stormy conditions and she cursed the weather under her breath. Every day without the sun was another day the *Libertas* was blindly sailing across a vast ocean. Without the sun, or the stars at night, navigation was difficult, if not impossible, and strong winds were not helping.

She sighed. Who was she kidding? They could be blown off course by a pace or a league and it probably wouldn't matter. They had no idea if they were heading in the right direction and no idea if Quinn was even still alive. Every day it became harder and harder for her to maintain her belief that her friend was okay.

"Stand straight," ordered Zain. "You all seem very lackluster today. A good morning for sparring, perhaps. Pair up."

Tomas assumed the fighting stance, fists held in front of his face. Ash didn't respond.

"Ash," said Zain. "Get ready to spar."

"What's the point? We're sailing into who knows where, we're hungry and we have no idea if it will ever end."

"You know why rations are short," said Zain. "We don't know when we will be able to restock. Now, assume the fighting stance."

She didn't move. "I don't want to."

"Ash, you are walking a thin line," said Zain.

"You have no feelings," she screamed. "Quinn could be dead!"

"Yes," said the captain. "He could. But what that has to do with your morning training, I am not sure."

"What's the point?" she repeated.

"It may save your life one day," said Zain. "Or someone else's."

"It didn't save Quinn's," she muttered.

"We don't know that."

She said nothing.

"Come on," said Tomas. "Stop behaving like such a girl."

Ash froze momentarily, before she recovered. "What did you say?" she blustered, trying to act offended, rather than worried.

"You're acting like a girl," said Tomas. "You don't often, but you are now."

Ash looked at Zain.

"You nearly had me fooled," Tomas went on, bouncing up and down in fighting stance, oblivious to the stir he was causing among the *Libertas* crew.

"Fooled?" said Zain.

"Yes, you know, she acts like a boy so well I thought she was one at first but –"

"What are you saying?" asked Jericho, pulling his moustache.

Tomas stopped bouncing. "Well, just that I worked out she's a girl – you all had me going for a while!"

Jericho looked at Zain, as the crew began to mutter and curse around them. "Captain?" he asked, tentatively.

Ash almost stopped breathing, waiting to hear what Zain would say next, knowing that it was his position as trusted leader on the line here, as much as her own. She also had a good idea of what would come next. He wouldn't lie to his crew. And he'd told her at the first meeting after she'd been discovered that he would do nothing to jeopardize this quest.

"Ash," the captain said calmly. "I think you can be excused this morning. Go and wait for me in Quinn's cabin."

Ash didn't need to be asked twice; she fled the deck, taking herself downstairs. "Get out," she said to Kurt, who was sitting at Quinn's desk, studying his map. He turned to her and said something in his strange, garbled Northern language. Ash frowned, wishing Quinn was there to tell the fox-faced boy off in Suspite or one of the many other languages he had learned.

She opened the door and pointed, her meaning clear. Kurt rolled his eyes, before slouching past her.

Ash closed the door, looking around the messy little cabin. It had not taken Tomas and Kurt long to assert ownership of the space. Kurt had commandeered the desk, leaving corks out of Quinn's precious colored inks and littering the top with stained quills and fingerprints. Tomas had scored Quinn's bed, which was unmade. Ash fingered the multicolored quilt he had thrown over the top, admiring the fine workmanship even as her tears threatened to spill.

She was in big trouble. Zain had told her that she could stay on board the *Libertas* as long as the crew didn't find out she was a girl. The superstitious seamen would not tolerate a female on board; centuries of tradition said that women (of any age) were bad luck.

If only Quinn were here, he might be able to convince them. He'd convinced Zain that there was no foundation to the tradition. She remembered he'd quoted some book to Zain about it being only a recent superstition, but she couldn't remember enough of the details to use it as any kind of defense.

She clenched her teeth, trying to keep the tears at bay. The last thing she needed was for a posse of angry sailors to come down here and find her crying.

Rain splattered against the porthole.

Ash tried to imagine what was going to happen to her. Hers was a "crime" punishable by death and the crew could vote to dump her overboard. Surely they wouldn't do that? They knew her now, and she knew them. She couldn't even conjure up a picture of Jericho, Abel, Cleaver and Ison making her walk the plank. And Zain? He would never allow it, she decided.

Hoped.

Agitated, Ash leapt to her feet. She wasn't going to sit here and wait to see what happened. If they were going to make her walk the plank, she would make them look her in the eye while they voted on it.

～

"We can't risk it," a deep voice was saying. "We don't know what we're sailing into and who knows how long it will take us to find Quinn."

Ash crept closer to the wheelhouse, around which the crew was clustered, talking intently.

"She's already been with us for months and nothing bad's happened. In fact, she patched me up!" said Abel.

"Nothing bad? Are you crazy? We saw a monster! Gelynions are chasing us! We were attacked!" replied Dilly.

A babble of conversation broke out at his words.

"I do not think we can blame Ash for the Gelynions," said Zain. "Nor for the attack."

"The monster then!" Dilly bellowed.

"Quinn is convinced that beast is good luck," said Cleaver. "He told me."

"Bah!" said Dilly. "It rears out of the water, blowing smoke. How is that good luck?"

"He's right," said Cook.

Ash, keeping track on her fingers, had two on the negative side, three on the positive. Several undecided.

She stepped forward.

"I know it's not proper that I'm here," she began, and there was a collective gasp as they turned to face her. "Then again," she continued, trying to sound relaxed, "my presence anywhere on board is unusual."

"Ash," Zain said, holding up a hand to stop her speaking.

"No, Zain," she said, lifting her chin. "I won't hide from this and I won't allow my fate to be decided by people who won't look me in the face. That happened to my mother – she was chased away from her home by cowards

137

in masks. Surely you are all brave enough to allow me to be here?" Her voice rose slightly on the last words.

Abel moved to stand beside her. "I am," he said.

"And I," said Cleaver.

"Aye," said Ison.

Dilly shuffled his feet and stared at the deck. Cook's eyes never left Zain's face. Kurt squinted at her.

Jericho paused. "I don't like the idea of a woman on board," he said, "but . . . I do like you. And you're just a slip of a girl really, so maybe it doesn't count."

Zain looked around at the circle of men. "All right, then, Ash," he said. "You may stay for the vote. Stand to one side."

"Wait," Ash interjected, fists clenched. "Kurt gets a vote? He's only been on board five minutes and he doesn't even speak Verdanian! Tomas is not here."

Zain nodded, his eyes betraying nothing of his thoughts. "Tomas chose to abstain," he said. "Kurt is an invited member of this company . . ."

Unlike you, Ash finished in her mind. After all, she'd begun her days on board as a stowaway.

"And he is a boy," Zain finished, softly.

Unlike you, Ash finished again.

"It's so unfair!" The words burst from her before she could stop them.

Zain moved towards her, and placed one hand on her shoulder, speaking so that only she could hear.

"Life is not fair, Ash," he said with the tone of one who was speaking from experience. "But you must have faith."

She opened her mouth to speak again, but closed it, realizing there was nothing she could say now. As difficult as it was to accept, she knew Zain was right.

Zain nodded before moving back to gather the crew around him in a circle. "We will use the silent method," he said. "One finger for yes, Ash stays and we go on as we are. Two for no, Ash must obey the laws of the sea."

Ash gulped, more aware than ever of the leagues of water around them. It was so blue, it looked solid, but she knew that she would plunge off the plank – down, down, down – with no hope of survival. She could feel tears welling behind her eyelids, but she blinked them back hard, determined to face her fate with courage.

"Now," said Zain, and Ash watched, mouth dry, as fingers popped up around the circle . . .

One. One. Two. One. Two. Two.

She could hardly breathe.

One.

The tang of the salty air around her was sharp; the sound of water lapping against the hull a soothing lullaby. Could she be taking her last breaths? Would that water soon be filling her ears for real?

One.

Relief crashed through her in such a wave that she thought she might fall.

"She stays," said Zain.

Overwhelmed with gratitude, Ash opened her mouth to speak, managing to forget for a moment the three votes against her, but Zain silenced her with a look.

"You will go below deck," he said. "And this time you will stay there until I call you. The rest of you, stay here."

Ash scurried away, feeling as though she might burst. She wanted to run and jump and sing and cry and wail and sleep and . . .

Cleric Greenfield appeared at the bottom of the stairwell. "Ah, Ash," he said. "Just the person. I had an idea about your plants – I thought we could talk."

The plants with the bright-red fruit that she'd found in the tribal village up north were a constant source of concern to her. She was desperate to keep them alive, so that she could do some further experiments with them upon her return to Verdania.

"Come on," said the cleric with a smile, and Ash couldn't help but smile back. He was a dear old thing, happy to sit and talk plants with her for hours. She'd learned a lot from him – and he from her. He brought book-learning to their conversations, and she brought practical knowledge, learned from her mam.

"I've thought of a way to preserve the seeds," the cleric was saying, opening the door wider. "Quite simple, really. If we squash a few of the fruits onto vellum and let them dry, we shall have nice little packets of seeds come the next growing season. I'm assuming we should sow in summer – they seem to respond well to the heat . . ."

Ash followed him down the passage as he talked, happy to allow herself to be distracted while she awaited a summons from Zain. Cleric Greenfield had been nowhere in sight up on the deck, but she wouldn't be surprised if he knew exactly what was going on. He didn't leave his cabin often but he always seemed to know when he was needed.

Chapter Nine

The bell had rung twice before Zain appeared at the open door of the cleric's cabin. "I thought I might find you here," he said. Ash was almost surprised to see him, so absorbed had she been in the work that she and Cleric Greenfield were doing. They had created several neat little packages and laid them on the cleric's windowsill to dry.

Ash stood to attention and braced herself for what was coming.

"Although the vote was split, all members of the crew will abide by it," said Zain, his tone serious. "However, I think it wise that you keep yourself to yourself for a little while."

"I will," she said. "And thank you."

"Don't thank me, thank Quinn," said Zain. "I used the information he quoted me from that book and it was enough to persuade the 'no' voters that it might not be fatal to keep you."

Mentally, she put in a word of thanks to Quinn – still there to save her, in spirit.

"I might add, however," Zain went on, "that the crew is as keen to see that book on our return as I am."

Ash gulped again, wondering whether Quinn could produce said book.

"You will always find a quiet space here," said Cleric Greenfield, gesturing around his cabin, "as Quinn did."

Zain and Ash both raised an eyebrow at that comment. But Ash also noted that the cleric asked no questions about Zain's words, which meant that he knew far more than he let on. As she'd always suspected.

"Shall we continue with our experiment?" he asked.

She nodded. The longer she could hide away down here with the cleric rather than face the crew, the better.

"I'll leave you to it then," said Zain. "But I'll expect you on deck for lunch, Ash. You can't hide down here forever."

He ducked out through the door, leaving her wondering once again if the captain was a mind reader.

～

Dilly, Cook and Kurt.

Ash rolled over onto her hip, staring out through the open door of the wheelhouse. After the longest afternoon of her life, she was finally tucked up in her sleeping roll, and it was only now that she allowed herself to think about the "no" votes.

Ash sighed aloud. Usually, when she felt lonely or confused or unhappy, she took solace in the stars. She would choose one, the brightest one, and talk to it as though it were her mam.

Tonight, there were no stars, and the *Libertas* bobbed almost motionless under the leaden skies. Zain had made the decision that evening to deploy the sea anchor, preventing the ship from drifting.

"There is no point in sailing onward when we cannot navigate," he'd told Cleaver, as Ash was readying her sleeping roll. "Hopefully, the sun will come out in the morning and we can fix our direction."

"Won't that delay our search for Quinn even further?" Ash couldn't help but ask.

"Perhaps," Zain admitted. "But sailing in the wrong direction will not further our cause."

She had nodded, sadly, and his face had softened. "All we have is hope, Ash," Zain said. "If you give that up, there is nothing."

So now she was lying in the gloomy dark trying to hope.

The one bright spark in her day had been Tomas. He had approached her at lunchtime, red-faced, tripping over his tongue, trying to apologize.

"I did not know it was important," he said, over and over again.

"Forget it," she said. "It was bound to come out sooner or later." Even as she'd said the words, she'd realized how true they were.

"I'm sorry," he said again, "you are a very good boy, you know. It took me a while to work it out . . ."

Out of the corner of her eye, she saw Jericho and Abel look at each other and grimace.

Suddenly she realized that half the problem was that the crew was embarrassed they hadn't twigged sooner.

"Look," she said, in a very loud voice. "Everyone knew. They're just better than you at keeping knowledge to themselves."

Jericho and Abel were nodding firmly.

"Ah," said Tomas, winking at her. "Of course."

After that, things had gone much more smoothly with the crew members who were still happy to sit with her. By the end of lunch, she could almost be forgiven for imagining that things were back to normal.

But of course they weren't.

"You need to be careful, Ash," said Cleaver, when she'd turned up in the wheelhouse that evening. She liked the gruff old sailor, and had spent many hours chatting easily with him in the past. "They'll be looking for reasons to blame you."

No need to mention who "they" were.

"Blame me for what?" she asked.

"Anything," he said. "Everything. I heard murmurings this afternoon that this blasted weather is your fault."

She burst out laughing.

"You can laugh," he said, face serious, "but you only squeaked through the vote this morning by a whisker. And doubt burns at the heart and the mind."

Now Ash's eyes searched the sky, looking for a sign, even the slightest twinkle of a star. She needed to talk to her mam.

But the inky blackness remained unbroken.

Turning her face to the wall, Ash tried to go to sleep. Things would be better in the morning. They had to be.

~

The rain fell like fine mist, so light that it barely moistened the skin. The *Libertas* rocked gently from side to side, and Ash knew that they were in for another day of little to no progress as the sea anchor dragged behind them, ballooning as it captured water. She almost wished that they were back in that strange, scary section of the ocean they'd hit a few days earlier, where the waves were wild and the *Libertas* was tossed about like a cork.

Fortunately, Tomas had been in the area before with his father. "It is always like this," he'd told Zain, above the roar of the waves. "Whether the skies be stormy or clear, the waves are always angry in this place."

Ash could only be grateful that they'd moved to calmer waters before she'd been discovered to be a girl – otherwise it would have probably been her fault that they'd all slipped and lurched around the deck for the better part of a day, as the waves played with their ship.

Now, the ocean was as flat as her mood.

A sudden shout from the bow roused her from her melancholy, and she sat bolt upright. Was it a sail? A ship? Quinn?

She jumped up and rolled her bedclothes neatly before stacking them in the corner. Ash knew she enjoyed a rare privilege by being able to sleep above deck in the fresh air, and in isolation. She made sure that Zain and Cleaver never had any reason to question her presence there.

She ran towards the bow, slipping on the wet deck in her bare feet.

"No boots?" Zain asked, as she approached. Ash grimaced. She knew that Zain believed that a sailor should never be without his boots, just in case.

"I was just –" she began, breathlessly. "Er, what are you doing?" He was standing beside Cleaver and Kurt, who looked immensely pleased with himself.

"Navigating," said Zain.

"What? How?" she blurted out. "There is no sun."

"With this," said Zain, holding out his hand. Nestled on his palm was a fragment of rock. She recognized it as the stone that Kurt often had in his hand – she'd assumed it was something he'd brought to remember his home.

"It's a rock," she said now.

Kurt mumbled something unintelligible, snatching the rock from Zain's hand and holding it up. Ash watched in fascination as the crystal hidden in the rock came to life, glowing with color.

"It's a sun stone," Zain said, as Kurt importantly moved the rock above his head. The colors faded as Kurt shifted the stone towards port and it glowed brightly again as he brought it back to its original position, radiating outward in circles. "It shows you where the sun is." Zain pointed to the center of the light circles. "Which means," he continued, "we can use the sun to find our direction – even when the sun is not visible."

"That's great," said Ash, trying to smile as Kurt watched her through narrowed eyes. She knew she should be excited – the revelation meant that they could haul in the sea anchor and set off after Quinn again. Only . . . two things bothered her.

The first was that Kurt's rock had given him such a big lift in Zain's estimation. Ash was not as suspicious of the Northern boy as Quinn had always been, but that didn't mean she trusted him. She had taken heart from the fact that Zain had always held him at arm's length, even as he'd tried to push his way into the role of mapmaker in Quinn's absence. She knew what it felt like to have no home and no parents and how desperate that could make a person – in her case, however, she'd always had Quinn, who was like family to her.

The second thing that bothered her was just *how long* it had taken Kurt to reveal his rock and what it could do. To think that he'd had it in his pocket the entire time that the *Libertas* had been drifting and Quinn was hurtling away from them to who knew where! It didn't bear thinking about and yet she knew it was important.

"Why didn't he tell us about this before?" she asked Zain.

But her question was lost in the ruckus of Cleaver arriving at the bow with Abel and Dilly in hot pursuit. "I've been telling the boys about the magic rock," Cleaver said, face wreathed in smiles. "Show them how it works."

As Zain indicated to Kurt to demonstrate the sun stone, Ash noticed Dilly moving as far away from her as possible. She frowned, suddenly feeling uncomfortable. As the sailors crowded around Kurt, she edged her way backward, out of the happy group.

All she could think of as she made her way to the stern of the ship was that Kurt's delay in sharing his sun stone meant that their chances of finding Quinn had diminished with every day.

Which, she suspected, is what Kurt had wanted all along.

Chapter Ten

Quinn watched the seabird flapping and cawing overhead as it circled the boat. Under normal circumstances, he'd have been thrilled by the sight of a bird because birds meant that land was not far away. But not today.

This bird was the one that Dinoh had released that morning from the cage behind the wheelhouse. And its return meant that land was not close enough for even a mighty flier such as this one to reach within a day.

Quinn sighed, knowing that soon he and Yergon would return to the black horror of the hold, to lie in silence until Morpeth arrived to collect them the following morning. Yergon had said little since those first words exchanged at the height of his panic about the waves. He had confided to Quinn the next day that he would not speak in the dark. "You cannot see the ears nearby," he'd said in a dramatic undertone.

Quinn supposed that a man who'd been so close to walking the plank had earned the right to be paranoid. He reached down and hitched his breeches up higher for the umpteenth time that morning. If he got any thinner, they'd be down around his ankles.

He squinted up at the setting sun, which had finally come out yesterday after four days of hiding behind cloud. At first, Quinn had applauded the lack of sun, assuming that it would slow the Gelynions down. Several overcast days had always given the *Libertas* cause to pause, Zain's caution about sailing leagues off course winning out over his desire to press forward and win the race.

It didn't take long for Quinn to realize, however, that not even this would slow down Juan Forden. With much ceremony, the explorer had strutted up on deck and demanded that a bird be released. And so Dinoh had thrown one poor feathered specimen off the bow, where it had hovered, confused for a while, before flying up in lazy circles.

From the deck, all eyes watched its progress – although Quinn's gaze switched between the bird and Juan Forden. As the bird's loops began increasing in size, Quinn noticed a small huddle of Gelynions in the stern. He sidled that way as far as his chain would allow and watched money change hands. The sailors were betting on something – which didn't surprise Quinn.

If there was one thing he'd learned while at sea, it was that sailors would bet on anything. The *Libertas* crew, for instance, played a complicated game involving a stack of very thin disks of wood marked with Deslondic symbols, over and over, in an endless marathon of winners and losers. They picked up and discarded cards in turn, and the idea was to bet that the value of symbols in your final hand would be closer to forty-two than anyone else's.

The Gelynions, however, had no disks in their hands. One man, standing watch over the others, eyes turned skyward, said a few sharp words, and all trading stopped. The men stood as one to watch the bird's wheeling flight – and when it suddenly darted off, one man, head wrapped in a dark red scarf, cheered while the others kicked their feet on the deck in frustration.

From what Quinn could tell, they'd been taking bets on which way the bird would fly. What he couldn't work out was why the bird had been let go.

He risked whispering the question to Yergon, who turned astonished eyes to him. "It will always go towards land," he said. "We follow. Have you never seen it before?"

Quinn shook his head, struck by the ingenuity of the concept. His first thought was how much he'd enjoy sharing the information with Zain. This was followed closely by the mood-dampening realization that he'd most likely never get the chance.

On and on through that first day they'd sailed, keeping the bird in sight. As evening fell, they lost it, swallowed up in the inky blackness that resulted when there was no moon and no stars. Not that Quinn had known. He'd been bundled down into the stale air of the hold by then, but in his mind's eye he could see the white silhouette of the bird like a beacon in the dark.

On land, he had a chance of escape. On land, there was somewhere to run. Here, even if he managed to break free of his cage or his chains, there was nowhere to go.

The following morning, Quinn had hurried up on deck as fast as he was able in the towering presence of Morpeth. He scanned the still-overcast skies, looking for a glimpse of the bird that had come to represent his freedom.

There was no sign of it.

"Where's the bird?" he'd asked Morpeth, trying to sound casual.

"The what?"

"You know, the bird."

Morpeth had laughed. "It fell out of the sky early this morning. Splash! Right under the bow of the ship. They fly until they die, you know, or until they reach land. In this case, death came first."

Quinn's heart sank.

"We'll send out another today," Morpeth continued, "but they're not for your entertainment. You have work to do. Now get to it!"

As Quinn settled to making meaningless marks on his charts, another bird was thrown out, and so it began once more. It was never the same again for Quinn, though. He came to realize that every one of those birds was as much a captive of the Gelynions as he was. Despite their ability to fly, they never managed to escape. And neither would he.

He looked now at the exhausted bird that had arrived back on deck. This one, at least, had had the sense to turn around for safety before it completely expired. The only one so far.

Quinn watched as Dinoh gathered it up, roughly shoving it back in the cage with the other birds, which shrieked and flapped, pecking at it with their hard yellow beaks. The returned bird, barely able to lift a wing in its own defense, scrambled backward into a corner. It would not be alive by morning, Quinn knew, as it tucked its head under its wing and pulled its legs under its feathers.

He also knew what would be on the menu for dinner the following night.

Quinn returned his attention to the map – Kurt's map, as he'd come to think of it. By labeling this one Kurt's and keeping the real map safely stored in his memory as his own, he'd been able to keep a clear picture of the differences between the two.

So far, there'd been little detail to add to either map during his time with the Gelynions. A situation that did not please Juan Forden.

"There is nothing happening here," he said not one bell later, surveying Quinn's map in his cabin. "You make no changes. You make no colors. You make *nothing*."

Morpeth's translation had been gleeful.

"I can only put what's there," said Quinn. "All we have seen so far is ocean."

"What is that then?" Forden put his finger on a dark smudge at the bottom of the map. Quinn was so distracted by the man's manicure that he missed the question when Morpeth asked it. Quinn looked down at his own grubby hands, with dirty, broken nails. Who was filing Forden's nails for him?

A sharp slap across the face with one of those manicured hands brought Quinn's focus back.

"Oh, er, I think it's an island," he said, tentatively touching his throbbing cheek, his hand coming away sticky with blood. Forden's heavy gold rings had left their mark. "I saw it this morning, only as a smudge on the horizon, a *suggestion* of land."

"The birds did not fly that way." It was a statement, not a question.

"No," agreed Quinn. "Perhaps I imagined it – but perhaps not. Your first mate, er, Dinoh, also looked that way, his eye caught by something."

155

"Bah!" said Forden, scratching at the smudge while Morpeth translated. "It is nothing."

Quinn winced at his casual violence towards the precious vellum.

"Wait, master," Morpeth said, slowly, in Gelynion. "What if there *is* something there? It is not far for us to have a look . . . and it would throw any Verdanian search party off our scent."

"Bah!" said Forden again. "We leave no scent. We disappeared into the night like a spirit wind . . ."

"True," said Morpeth, appearing to Quinn to choose his words carefully. "But if the Verdanian aristocrat double-crossed his own countrymen, what would he do to his Gelynion *friends*?"

As Forden considered this, Quinn tried very hard to look as though he did not understand a word, but his mind was racing. He had no idea of the size of the land he'd seen, but if the *Black Hawk* docked there, his chances of escape went from zero to . . . well, who knew, but anything more than zero was an improvement.

"We could, er, ask Dinoh if he saw anything," Quinn ventured, in Suspite. "That way we would know for sure whether to remove it from the map or not."

Forden's eyes moved from him to Morpeth, who was nodding. "Very well," he sighed. "Perhaps there will be treasure there for me to shower on our beloved Queen."

Quinn wished Ash was with him, though in that wish he was not tethered to the deck of the *Black Hawk*, but rather leaning over the rail of the *Libertas*, pointing out the white sand of the beach, the pale turquoise of the water, and the bright splashes of color dotting the lush, green foliage that fringed the picture. The *Black Hawk* was anchored about one hundred paces from the beach, and even that was a little close – Quinn could hear a scraping sound near the bow that suggested sand beneath the wood.

There was no sign of any settlement near the shore, but Quinn wasn't too worried, remembering the tribal village the *Libertas* had stumbled upon, well hidden behind a forest of trees.

The only questions he had about this land were a) how big it was and b) how he was going to get to it. Forden was organizing a landing party, herding sailors into a longboat, but it didn't look as though Quinn and Yergon were included.

Quinn thought fast. He had to get himself into that boat if he had any chance of escaping. For that was what he planned to do. With any luck, this beach was just a headland, leading to a broad, wide land beyond. A broad, wide land full of people and ships and somebody willing to take Quinn to Verdania. He wasn't entirely sure how he was going to convince someone to do that, but he'd worry about that when the time came – after all, he wasn't entirely sure how he was going to escape from the *Black Hawk* either.

"Ahem," he said now, clearing his throat loudly as Morpeth strolled past. The big Deslonder was showing no sign of lining up for shore duty, which was another plus as far as Quinn was concerned. The more distance he put between himself and Morpeth the better.

"It might be a good idea if I were to go ashore," Quinn said, trying to sound like it didn't matter either way.

"Oh," said Morpeth, raising his eyebrow in that way that reminded Quinn of Zain. "And why is that?"

"Well, er, I could see if I could find a vantage point to, er, better render the coastline," said Quinn. "It's the best way to get the detail."

"I see," said Morpeth. "And would you not agree that the view from here is very clear?"

They both turned to stare across the deck at the inviting beach.

"Well, er, yes," Quinn stumbled. "But . . . the lie of the land can be so much more obvious from an elevated position like – that one." His desperate, searching eyes had come to rest on a rocky knoll at one end of the sand.

"Indeed," said Morpeth. He studied Quinn for a long moment before adding, "No."

Watching Morpeth stroll across the deck, laughing to himself, Quinn wanted to stamp his feet in frustration.

"What is it?" said Yergon, looking up from his place on the deck beside Quinn. Unlike Quinn, the Gelynion hadn't even stood up to survey the inlet in which they were anchored. He had become paler, thinner and quieter with every passing day of their journey.

"I want to go ashore," said Quinn. "I need to get off this ship." He tried to make it sound as though he just needed to stretch his legs on solid ground, but from the close look that Yergon gave him, he knew he hadn't convinced the Gelynion.

And yet Yergon nodded. "Leave it to me," he said.

He stood up and began pacing back and forth, stretching his tether towards the bow, sighing, and walking towards the stern and doing the same, appearing to grow more agitated with each step.

"What are you doing?" Quinn hissed, as he realized that all movement on deck had come to a halt as each person turned to watch Yergon, who was now groaning and tearing his hair out.

Yergon didn't respond, and his actions continued to grow wilder until he screamed and threw himself on the deck, as though praying to a god.

Quinn stared down at him.

"What are you doing?" asked Morpeth, repeating Quinn's words. He stood over Yergon, with one toe of his boot lifting Yergon's chin.

"It's Dorada," Yergon screamed. "Dorada!"

The men on board drew breath as one, a sound of hope and fear.

But Morpeth laughed. "Don't be ridiculous," he told Yergon. "Dorada does not exist."

This time the Gelynions muttered angrily, and Morpeth appeared to realize that he'd said the wrong thing. "Not in an earthly sense," he went on hurriedly. "It is a land of spiritual reward."

Yergon stood up, eyes blazing, and Quinn almost stepped back, away from his intensity. "Where the crescent moon –" Yergon stopped and indicated the curve of beach. "Meets the silken sky." A sweep of the hand across the blue ocean. "Meets the bounty of earthly delights." By the time Yergon pointed to the lush cushion of vegetation on the fringe of the sand, the other Gelynions had crowded around and were all nodding enthusiastically, following Yergon's hand movements eagerly. "And there ye shall find the sun's prize." Yergon's voice rose, and suddenly the crowd was cheering.

Quinn shook his head in wonder. What was going on?

"You think there is gold here," Morpeth said, sounding amused. "More gold than we can imagine."

Yergon nodded. "It fits the description," he said, sounding a lot calmer now that he'd gotten his message across.

"It certainly does," said Forden's voice from the back of the crowd. "It is a wonder I did not see it myself. Perhaps it is a good thing we did not feed you to the sharks after all, Yergon."

Yergon said nothing.

Forden clapped his hands twice, a signal for attention. "Our plans change," he said. "We will all go ashore. And we will not leave until we have found enough gold to fill the *Black Hawk*."

Quinn had a sudden image of the ship sinking beneath the weight of the gold.

"Well, perhaps enough to fill your cabin, sire," said Morpeth, who appeared to be having the same thought.

Forden laughed. "Always so cautious, Morpeth," he said, waggling his moustache at the Deslonder in glee. "But if I bring back to Rey Bernardino the map marking the location of Dorada, I will be able to build ships from my gold. Houses from my gold! Villages from my gold! And the Queen will make me her number one advisor."

Morpeth sighed. "Very well, sire."

"Come then – we go!" said Forden. "Bring Yergon and the mouse as well. Let us see if he digs as well as he draws."

As Dinoh bent down to unhook their tethers, Yergon looked over at Quinn and winked.

The fine sand ran through his fingers like water, and Quinn sighed in frustration. This was the fourth hole he'd dug on the beach, and he was no closer to working out how to escape than when he'd first set foot on the sand. He'd managed to work his way closer to the thick, deep undergrowth, but the sun was now sliding towards the horizon and he estimated that he had only two bells before the dark would drop down on them from above.

If he was going to move, it had to be now.

All around him, Gelynions were digging like crazy men. No matter that the holes they dug collapsed continuously and revealed nothing but more sand. No matter that the sun beat down on them, or that grit got in their eyes and up their noses. They were convinced there was gold here, and each of them was determined to be the man to find it.

Juan Forden, of course, was not digging. Instead, he and Morpeth lounged in the longboat, calling for water occasionally, deep in conversation. Quinn watched now as they both turned to look out to sea, staring at the horizon.

Quinn did not stop to follow their gaze, choosing to glance around him instead. All other eyes were focused on the sand.

This was it. Now or never.

Quinn began to ease slowly backward, reaching out behind him with his feet, feeling for the shiny, thick leaves he'd been eyeing for what felt like days. A Gelynion sailor looked up, and Quinn began frantically digging, smiling at the sailor, pointing to the sand. The sailor sneered in response, then lowered his head once more, concentrating on his own task.

Quinn bit his lip as he felt his left foot disappear into the plants, one thick leaf lying like a wet cloth across the gap between his boot and his breeches, pulled up by his prone position. He shuddered, thinking of sliding into that moist, dense wall, wondering what might be in there. Could it be worse than what was out here?

He looked around at the Gelynions, considered the fact that if he stayed here, he'd be going home to Gelyn with them – if they didn't dump him overboard as soon as they had no further use for him.

No. Nothing in the trees could be as bad as this.

With that thought in mind, he slithered the last few paces across the sand and into the greenery. He just wished he hadn't left Ash's knife rolled up in his blanket below deck that morning.

~

Beyond the beach this land was rotten. It was like a pear that looked perfect, but squished in your mouth and filled it with granules of sour, brown flesh. Quinn was covered in spikes and prickles, small black slugs had attached themselves to his hands and he was hopelessly lost in a hot, steamy thicket. Moisture seemed to rise out of the ground here, coating him and making his clothes heavy and scratchy.

Behind him, he could hear the Gelynions shouting to each other as they tracked him through the trees. Fortunately for him, the plants were supple here, they simply sprang back into place behind him, so he left no broken trail. Unfortunately for him, the dense walls of greenery made it hard to see the sun – he had no idea how far he'd come or in what direction he was traveling. Somewhere nearby he could hear a low roaring noise, suggesting a river or stream. He was aiming for that sound, hoping it might lead him to a settlement. To something.

It hadn't taken the Gelynions long to realize he was missing from the beach. He reckoned he was no more than fifty or sixty paces ahead of them. But if it was hard going in here for him – a not-too-large boy – it must have been torture for the bigger men. At least he could duck under some of the low-hanging branches – they must be constantly walking into them, and so many of them seemed to be covered in thorns.

Quinn felt a bite on his hand and looked down to see another of those infernal slugs. He pried if off, wondering what they were. Every time he pulled one off, it seemed bigger than the previous one, and a few drops of his blood followed. He had a very uncomfortable feeling they were feeding on him.

He pushed past a tall, thin tree covered in vines, and found himself up to his boot tops in water. The stream was wide and eerily beautiful, filtered sunlight reflecting from the mist thrown off by the rapidly rushing water. Though fast, it didn't look too deep.

Lifting one sodden boot, Quinn felt the suck of mud underfoot as he stepped forward into the white water. He paused, trying to gauge the speed and depth of the water, when he felt a strange sensation up the inside of his boots.

Looking down, he saw a flash of silver through the bubbles. Then another. Fish, he thought, admiring the play of light on their scales as they moved.

Fish, another part of his brain thought, moving back through his memory to a picture of Tomas holding up his finger. "*Pescarn*. You never meet *one* of them. Always more, ten, twenty . . . and they will eat the flesh off your bones in minutes."

Quinn's eyes widened as he saw that the flash of silver had become a lightning storm around his boots. That strange sensation was a tugging as the shoal of fish *tried to eat his boots.*

Desperately, he turned and clutched at a vine hanging overhead, pulling himself out of the water. It snapped under his weight, and he tumbled into the river, sitting in the mud, with water – and *pescarn* – up to his waist.

The fish were swarming around him and he could feel sharp pinpricks through his thick breeches. Stunned, he grabbed at the nearest fish, whipping his hand back in horror as it opened its rubbery mouth to reveal a double set of razor-sharp fangs that seemed to take up half its small body. The teeth snapped together a hair's breadth from his little finger.

He had to get out of here!

Quinn scrambled to his feet, realizing that the *pescarn* were gripping on for dear life, their bodies wriggling in the air. Surely they were like any other fish, needing water to breathe? But no, they seemed more interested in *eating him* than breathing!

He could hear the Gelynions tramping closer through the undergrowth. If he stepped back through the vines, they would see him. If he stayed where he was, there'd be nothing left of him. Even as he brushed the *pescarn* from his legs, they were trying to taste the flesh on his hands, and more and more were gathering around his boots.

Quinn grimaced. Tomas's advice for dealing with the *pescarn* comprised mostly "avoid them," or throwing some meat in the water to distract them. Given there was no random carcass lying about, he needed to avoid them. He took three quick steps to the trunk of the tree, and began to climb, his wet breeches and boots causing him to slip and slide along the smooth bark. Sharp pinpricks of pain ricocheted up his legs as the tiny *pescarn* chewed their way through his breeches and began to gnaw his flesh. He thumped one leg, then the other, against the trunk in an attempt to dislodge them, but succeeded only in adding bruises to the bite marks. The entire tree shimmied and shook with his movements, causing the curtain of vines to wave softly, and there was a loud squawk and a bright flash of dazzling red and yellow as a bird overhead took fright and then flight.

Startled, Quinn nearly lost his grip on the trunk, before gritting his teeth and inching upward. If he was in the tree, chances were he could escape both his predators. The Gelynions would not see him, the fish would surely die any minute now without air. Perhaps the fish would solve all his problems and eat Juan Forden . . .

He reached a wide fork in the tree and settled into it, pulling the remaining *pescarn* from his breeches and boots by the tail and flinging them down to the lake below. His boots had several chunks torn from the top, but at least the leather had stopped the *pescarn* tearing flesh from his feet. His breeches were ripped in a dozen places, and he found himself thankful for his mam's sewing lessons – given a needle and thread, he'd be able to repair them.

Quinn rolled his eyes. Here he was, sitting in a tree in the middle of who knew where, contemplating needlework. He could just imagine Ash's response to that.

Quinn wiggled around in his seat, realizing that he was high enough here to get an idea of the landscape. Turning his head left and right, then back again, his heart sank. He was surrounded on all sides by dense, green walls of trees. Looking behind him, he could just make out the beach he'd come from, though the glare on the sand was much dimmer now that the sun was going down.

Ahead of him, the sea of trees seemed to continue about the same distance – before ending at what Quinn suspected was another beach.

He rested his head against the trunk of the tree, blinking back the bitter disappointment that rose within him. He was on an island. And not a very large one at that.

There would be no escaping the Gelynions today.

"Ah, there you are."

Morpeth's voice rose up from below. Quinn looked down into his face, which was gratifyingly close to the lake's edge. For one moment, Quinn had a crazy image of dropping down on the Deslonder's head, tackling him sideways into the lake and the jaws of the awaiting *pescarn*. It was only the blood on his breeches and the memory of those painful bites that stopped him acting on it – if Morpeth went into the water, so would Quinn, and it would be an excruciating way to die.

"We have been searching for you, Monstruo Mouse," said Morpeth, taunting him. "You disappeared in such a hurry . . . though where you thought you were going, we have no idea." He indicated the dense landscape, a cruel smile on his face.

"Oh, I . . ." Quinn thought fast. The truth was, he needed to get back on the *Black Hawk* now, as much as he hated to admit it. The alternative was to stay here and die. "I was looking for a better place to dig for gold," he began, trying to come up with a believable story.

"Indeed," said Morpeth, mouth still smiling while his eyes were flat and cold. "Up a tree?"

"Ye-e-es," said Quinn, looking around desperately for inspiration. "I thought I might get a better, er, lie of the land here – for gold and for the map."

"Get down," said Morpeth, all pretense at good humor gone. "There is no gold here. There is nothing here. We are wasting our time and you, Monstruo Mouse, are wasting it more than anyone. We are all covered in bites and bugs and slugs because of you, Monstruo, and we will not easily forget that."

Shivering, Quinn began to ease his way back down the trunk. There was nothing else for it.

"No," Morpeth repeated. "We will not forget."

~

Quinn marked another day on his cage, guessing in the dark where best to put it. He'd added three marks since his return to the *Black Hawk*, wrapped in rope, legs bleeding, feeling defeated, and his mood was as black as the air around him.

Forden had decreed that he would not see daylight until the captain felt that he'd paid the right price for his "adventure." In the meantime, Yergon was up on deck, making notes for the map.

Worse than his banishment to the dark, however, was the knowledge that the *Libertas* had sailed right past that island while he was digging for nonexistent gold and failing to escape. Morpeth had taken great pleasure in relaying that information as Quinn was climbing back into the hold, wincing at the pain of the bites on his legs.

"Oh, Monstruo," he'd said, tone friendly. "By the way, we saw your friends . . . Well, from a distance."

Quinn had frozen in position on the rope ladder, heart racing. Was that what had caught Forden's attention, giving Quinn the opportunity to slither off into the trees?

"Yes," Morpeth went on, quite as though they were discussing the weather. "Raced right past us. Anyone would think they were chasing something . . ."

His laugh was loud and cruel. "Ironic, really. As we were chasing you, they were sailing away. All you did with your stupid antics was to put them farther in front. They will never find you now!"

With that, he'd dropped the trapdoor, leaving Quinn to fumble his way down the ladder in the dark, heart in his boots, knowing Morpeth was right. His friends had been trying to find him, they hadn't given up. But the *Libertas* would never look behind them for Quinn. Why would they?

He shifted gingerly to lie on his back in the dark. The bites on his legs had crusted over and were no longer bleeding, which was a good thing, but they were still uncomfortable. He could only be thankful that there was no sign of infection.

A sudden crash overhead thundered through his self-pity and brought him to a sitting position. What was that? Stomping in the passageway above suggested running feet, and he could hear a strange scraping noise down the starboard side of the *Black Hawk*.

Straining his ears, he could just make out the sound of men shouting over the slap of waves hitting the hull. Over time, he'd become used to the splash of the water, so much louder down here on the waterline than it was in his cabin on the *Libertas*, but in the first few days it had nearly driven him mad.

Then came the ringing sound of steel on steel . . .

Quinn slid Ash's knife from his boot and came to a crouch as the sounds from above intensified into the unmistakable noise of men fighting. Not just fighting – *battling*.

Someone had boarded the *Black Hawk*. Could it be Zain? Had he somehow spotted the *Black Hawk*?

Behind him? Quinn's brain whispered. *Not likely.*

Then someone else. Dolan? Odilon? At this point Quinn would be happy to see even those two again, despite his dislike of them. Odilon would bring Ajax, and he was someone Quinn could rely on. And surely even Ira wouldn't simply leave him here . . . Quinn's brow furrowed as he thought about that. *Maybe he would.*

One thing was certain – nobody was going to go looking for Quinn down here in the dark. He needed to get up on deck to see what was happening.

For the first time in three days, Quinn hoped that nobody would open the trapdoor above him. The last thing Quinn needed right now was to be bathed in a shaft of blinding light.

Satisfied that none of the shouts and pounding feet he could hear were coming from the passage above his head, he crept from the cage. When he'd first been aboard, they'd used a complicated knotting system to ensure that he couldn't simply untie himself. Then they'd downgraded to a conventional seaman's knot. Now they didn't even lock the door. Clearly the Gelynions had realized, as he had, that even if he managed to get out of the cage, he had nowhere to go.

Until now.

Quinn quickly made his way to the bottom of the rope ladder.

He paused again – still no sounds directly overhead – and scrambled up the ladder, feeling for the rungs.

Wafer-thin slivers of light outlined the square of the trapdoor. When he got to the top, he reached up and pushed hard against the solid wood. It didn't move.

Sweating, with the rope ladder swinging beneath him, he took another step up the ladder and tried to put one shoulder against the door, neck and head craned awkwardly to one side, as he pushed with all the force he could muster. He felt the wood lift slightly, but it would not open.

"*Leif's boots!*" he muttered, stepping back down the ladder, and looking up at the trapdoor. Why wouldn't it open? He'd never noticed an obvious lock on the trapdoor when Morpeth or one of the others was pushing him and Yergon down through it at the end of the day. What could the problem be? He could feel his heart racing with the effort of pushing – and the fear of being caught, exposed, on this ladder should someone open the trapdoor from above.

He wiped one sweaty palm on his breeches before replacing it on the ladder and wiping the other. As he did so, Quinn remembered Cleaver's advice to him during those first days on board the *Libertas* – one hand for you, one for the ship – and smiled wryly. That Quinn, green about the gills and wishing he was at home in his bedroom, would never have imagined he'd find himself up a rope ladder, in the dark, on a Gelynion ship.

But if he ever wanted to see his bedroom again, this Quinn needed to find a way to get through this trapdoor.

Carefully, swaying back and forth on the ladder, he reached for the knife in his boot and turned back to the trapdoor. Slipping the knife into the light slivers, he worked it around first one side, then another. It was on the third side that the knife hit an obstacle with a soft thunk.

Thinking hard, Quinn flicked back through his memory, looking for pictures of the passage and the trapdoor. He knew there was no obvious lock, hasp, ring or bolt. What then? Was there something that could be secured across the trapdoor once the prisoners were inside? He shook his head. He would remember the sound of it being put in place if that had been the case.

It wasn't until his memory dredged up an image of that first morning on board that he saw it. A ridge of wood, located about a hand width from the far side of the trapdoor. He had thought nothing of it – the passage had regularly spaced wooden slats, designed to give footholds in rough seas – but now he saw that this one was not dead straight, as would be expected. Instead, it was on a strange angle, as though it was designed to turn on a screw and secure the trapdoor.

With renewed vigor, Quinn attacked the trapdoor, sliding his knife back and forth to push hard against the obstacle.

Thunk. Thunk. Thunk.

And then there was a tiny squeak as the wood shifted. Two slides later, the obstacle was gone, and Quinn lifted the trapdoor carefully, climbing up the ladder so that he could peer into the passage. Nothing moved, though now that he was closer he could hear the Gelynions still running about the deck. He pushed the trapdoor open and clambered out, knife in hand.

A sharp, metallic clang rang through the air, confirming for Quinn that Forden had decided to greet his visitors – whoever they were – with steel. Given the superior numbers of the Gelynion crew, he could only hope Ajax wasn't trying to fight his way on board.

The closer he got to the steps to the deck, the louder and more ferocious the noise of the battle became. It sounded as though fifty men were up on deck, shouting and swearing, as swords clanged and the sea roared around them. But how could there be that many? No Verdanian crew was that big.

Frowning, Quinn wondered if he should run up the stairs, knife held high and join in. Or . . . he remembered the approach the *Libertas* crew took when faced with an unknown situation, such as when they'd come across Odilon's deserted camp in a quiet cove up north. They'd gone in quietly until they were in position and then pitched themselves into the camp, making enough noise for twenty men.

So be it.

Quinn crept up the stairs towards the light, sliding onto his stomach for the last few steps to keep his head down. Slowly, quietly, he raised himself far enough above deck level to get an idea of what was happening.

And blinked.

The deck was teeming with sailors, but none of them were Verdanian. Wild-looking men, long haired and bare-foot, were dressed in a ragtag collection of clothes and hats – some in breeches, some in robes similar to what Frey had worn. The most unified thing about them, apart from the weapons they were brandishing with glee, was the gold that dripped from them. Necklaces, rings, earrings – one who wore an eye patch even had a mouthful of gold teeth, glinting in the sun when he smiled. Which he was doing as he swung a long, thin sword at Dinoh.

Pirates!

Quinn ducked his head back down below deck level, thinking fast. Overhead, he could hear Forden shouting orders at his men and then a huge, deep roar as Morpeth threw himself into battle somewhere near the stern of the ship.

What should he do?

Going up on deck meant certain death. He could not see how the Gelynions, even as fierce as they were, could possibly out fight more than twice their number of heavily armed men. And what could he, one pre-growth-spurt boy, do to change that?

But going back to the hold to hide in the dark was not an option either. The pirates would search the entire ship looking for treasure and supplies, and the hold, with its many boxes and crates and barrels, would be one of the first places they'd look. If he was going to die, better it be quick and with honor than slow and crouched in the dark like the mouse that the Gelynions thought he was.

Quinn fingered his knife, which now felt small and fragile in his hand. His mind raced, desperate thoughts of what to do interspersed with flashes of memory – his mam and da, his brothers, Zain, Ash, Ajax – all swirling around like the ribbons on the maypole.

Quinn crawled up onto the deck on his stomach. He needed a better perspective from which to view the fighting. Forden and Morpeth were occupied towards the bow, back-to-back, fighting off pirates. Quinn got up onto his haunches and scurried across the deck to the nearest mast, climbing it faster than he'd ever climbed before. From the lookout, he surveyed the ship below him, noting the pirate ship tied alongside, with more pirates swarming on board even now.

It wouldn't be long before the Gelynions were overpowered.

Quinn's breath came in shallow gasps as he tried to think his way through this mess, eyes desperately scanning the horizon, searching for inspiration.

And that's when he saw it. Far ahead, in the distance, a ship, sailing away from him.

Three masts – so not the *Fair Maiden* or the *Wandering Spirit*. The *Libertas*? It had to be!

Quinn's spirits soared – then crashed like an exhausted seabird on the deck. The *Libertas* was sailing *away* from him. And he was on a ship that was rapidly becoming a battlefield, with no escape.

Quinn's jaw tightened, his eyes following the progress of the ship in the distance.

He needed to attract its attention. But how?

And then it came to him. There was only one thing that would be seen for leagues on an ocean this vast – and that was fire.

Fire, on a wooden boat, in the middle of an endless ocean. Risky, he acknowledged to himself, but what was the alternative? To die at the hands of pirates? To continue his journey to Gelyn as a captive?

No, it was all or nothing.

Quinn shimmied down the mast as fast as he could. He had a plan now, and nothing was going to stop him. As he made his way to the stairs, he noticed that the pirate's ship was tied alongside the *Black Hawk*, ready for a quick getaway. Dropping to a crouch, Quinn ran towards it, barely daring to breathe.

He untied the rope, then looped it loosely around the rail so that to the casual observer it would still appear to be firm, but would be much easier for him to remove in a hurry. He just hoped the loop would hold until he got back.

Even on a day like this, when the calmness of the ocean and the stillness of the clear blue sky were so at odds with the chaos on the *Black Hawk*, the natural drift of the ocean would work to pull the pirate ship gently away from the rail.

Quinn knew he didn't have long – and he had work to do.

Sliding back down the stairs, he landed with a thump at the bottom and then scurried down the passage to Forden's cabin. It was unlocked, as he'd hoped, obviously abandoned as the reality of the foreign ship's identity became clear and Forden rushed upstairs to defend the *Black Hawk*. Lying on top of the desk was Quinn's map.

Quinn ran to the other side of the desk and scrabbled through the drawers, throwing quills and ink to the floor in his haste. But he couldn't find what he was looking for.

He turned desperate eyes to the rest of the cabin. A box of wine. A pile of coins. A gutted candle beside the bed . . .

Quinn hurried to the candle. And there it was. Flint and a firestone.

With shaking hands, he bashed them together, trying to spark the wick in the stubby candle. He held his breath as a tiny flame flickered, only to die almost instantly.

Frustrated, he struck the flint and firestone again, over and over.

Lots of sparks, but no flame.

"*Leif's boots!*" he cursed. Ajax was right. He really needed a new oath. Leif and his boots were not strong enough for a moment like this.

He walked away from the candle, trying to calm his shaking nerves, and then approached again. This time, he struck more precisely, and breathed gently outward at the same time, fanning the tiny spark into an equally tiny flame.

The wick sputtered and winked before his eyes, and then settled, gathering strength and burning brightly. The strong fishy smell and black smoke that arose from it told Quinn that even world-famous Gelynion explorers burned the cheapest candles available. Mesmerized, Quinn had almost forgotten that there was a fight raging on deck until a mammoth crash overhead brought him back to his senses.

Protecting the flame with his hand, he paused at the desk to grab the map and shove it down the front of his shirt. Glancing around, he thought ruefully of the information that was held within these walls, and how much he would like to exploit his current, unfettered access.

But there was no time.

Carefully shielding his little flame, Quinn headed back towards the steps. Peeking above the deck line again, he could see that his prediction was right. The Gelynions were on the back foot and the pirates would soon take control of the *Black Hawk*.

There was only one thing to do, and he needed to do it before his nerve failed.

Pulling the map from his shirt, Quinn gazed upon it one last time. Even though it was a fake, he had still put work into it and what he was about to do was going to hurt. Taking the candle, he held the flame to the corner of the vellum, watching as it took hold and then, in a quick puff, he blew out the candle.

As quickly as he dared, hand shielding the little flame, he made his way back to the mast.

Quinn's eyes widened at the carnage now around him. There were at least six Gelynions lying unmoving on the deck, blood pooled around them. The deck was slick with water and sweat and blood. The sound of the melee drowned out the lapping of the waves. He put his head down, keeping a close eye on the corner of the map, which had now burst into flame. He didn't have long.

It felt like a year before he reached his goal, and included a brief stop to open the door to the birdcage, but finally Quinn was standing against the masts. With one hand holding the map, his progress up the mast was awkward, and he'd just made it past the boom when he heard a shout and looked down to see one of the pirates pointing at him.

He wasn't as high as he'd like, but there was no time to waste. Quinn held the burning map against the sail.

"Come on, come on," he muttered, one eye on the flame, which seemed to be dithering about what to do next, and one eye on the pirate who was now running towards him. "Come on!" Quinn shouted, exhorting the flame to get on with it.

It seemed to listen to him for it suddenly caught the sail and exploded upward, ripping across the fabric like a golden arrow. The heat took Quinn by surprise – he hadn't expected the sail to go up so fast! He instinctively moved backward, away from the fire – and fell right off the mast.

As he plummeted towards the deck, Quinn realized that it was probably a good thing he'd not managed to get any higher.

And then he landed with a thud, and the world went black.

Chapter Eleven

"Smoke, astern."

Ash turned, startled. Jericho was on watch and the last time he'd seen "smoke" a huge, white monster had reared up out of the ocean, terrifying everyone. Except Quinn, she thought with a smile, who'd decided the beast was a good luck charm.

Maybe this meant their luck had changed?

She could only hope, for the past week on the *Libertas* had been like a bad dream for her. With half the crew still avoiding her and the other half trying to work out how to treat her now that she was a girl, she missed Quinn more than ever.

"Astern?" she heard Zain shout back.

"Astern. Smoke," the watch confirmed. "And lots of it."

Not Quinn's monster then, Ash thought, disappointed. "How far?"

"Two leagues," came the response.

Ash shivered. Fire at sea was every sailor's nightmare. Before, when the crew had been treating her like one of them, they'd loved sharing their horror stories with her and Quinn. She'd listened with that same delicious shiver of fear and anticipation she'd had when Quinn's brothers had told them ghost stories. But the reality was that fire on board a ship meant almost certain death for all hands.

She hoped it wasn't the *Fair Maiden* – she had no love for Odilon but she didn't want Ajax at risk. She wouldn't even wish horror like that on the *Wandering Spirit*.

"Ready about," called Zain, in a booming voice that could be heard all over the *Libertas*, and each crewmate responded, "Ready."

A creaking sound overhead heralded the change in direction, as the sails were angled across the wind and the *Libertas* slowly turned about.

"Ship ho!" called Jericho, indicating that they were now on course for the burning vessel. "Dead ahead."

"Trim the sails," ordered Zain. From her position on the rail, Ash could see him squinting at the horizon, mentally calculating sail angles and wind direction. The breeze began to lift the ends of her hair as the *Libertas* picked up speed.

She went to the wheelhouse to stand by Zain. He was leaning forward over the wheel, as though willing the ship to go faster.

"Will we make it in time?" she asked.

Zain looked at her briefly, before turning his gaze back to the ocean. Without Jericho's elevated advantage, they could only just see wisps of smoke on the horizon.

"I hope so," said Zain. "I hope so."

They stood in silence, eyes locked on the smoke. Cook rang the dinner bell.

"Eat," said Zain. "You will need your strength. If we get there in time, we may need your healing skills."

Ash shuddered, not sure if it was the "if" or the idea of what they might find that worried her most.

"Er, do you think . . . that is . . ." She stopped, unable to voice her biggest fear.

"Is it Quinn Freeman?" asked Zain, eyes steady ahead. "If it is, I will want to hear how the *Black Hawk* came to be behind us. Until then, we can only prepare. Now eat."

Silently, Ash left the wheelhouse and made her way to the galley, where Cook slopped some gruel in a bowl for her without a word. She took it to the bow and ate, tasting nothing, eyes on the smoke that seemed no closer.

⁓

Rough wood beneath his cheek, the smell of smoke, an uncomfortable heat from above . . . As Quinn's world came into focus, he remembered where he was. And what he'd done.

Quinn opened one eye, gasping in agony as light triggered a thudding pain in his head. He tried to lift it, but gave up when the movement set off dizzying starbursts of hurt. Maybe he'd just lie here a little longer . . .

As though from afar, he could hear Forden shouting at his Gelynions to bring water. The pirates were screaming at each other, but Quinn couldn't understand a word.

Quinn smiled to himself. It sounded as though his plan had worked. The smoke had caused enough confusion on board to stop the carnage – for now. And, with any luck, Zain would see it.

Eyes closed, he contemplated briefly the scenario where Zain failed to look behind him and was this very minute sailing gaily over the horizon towards Verdania . . . but he banished the thought a second later. It was time to work on the next part of his plan, in which he crept over to the pirate ship, threw himself on board and sailed gaily off towards the horizon by himself.

As plans went, it was . . . piecemeal. But it was all he had at this point.

Quinn rolled onto his back and stared straight up at blue sky and billowing smoke. Where exactly was he?

Gingerly, he attempted to raise his head again, fighting the dizzying waves as he turned to the left – for a clear view of the horizon. He looked right, which brought about another burst of pain. Through a curtain of eye-watering smoke, he could see Gelynions and pirates alike dropping buckets on ropes over the side of the ship, hauling in water.

In the one piece of good luck he'd had in weeks, Quinn realized the wheelhouse roof had broken his fall from the mast. If it hadn't, he'd be feeling considerably worse than the "awful" he felt right now.

Breathing shallowly, he rolled gently towards the mast and peered over the side – before jerking back again seconds later when he realized he was looking down at the top of Juan Forden's thick, black hair.

"Faster, you idiots!" he was screaming. "Do you all want to die?"

Even above the chaotic noise of the fire, shouting in many languages and the trampling feet, Quinn could hear Forden pacing angrily back and forth. "When I find the moron who did this he will be mincemeat! *Mincemeat!*"

Quinn gulped.

He heard the rumble of Morpeth's voice and craned to hear.

"This was not done by one of us," he said. "No one on this ship would be so stupid."

"Well, *someone was!*"

"A stupid pirate," blustered Morpeth. "Look at them! So stupid that they now take orders from the man they were fighting."

"Bah!" said Forden. "Kill them all."

"We shall . . . just as soon as they've helped us put out this fire."

A *crack!* overhead split the air. Quinn watched horrified as the top portion of the mast broke away, falling to the deck in a stream of flames and sparks. A man screamed and then wailed in agony, as sailors ran for cover.

"That's one less we have to kill," said Morpeth.

"Shut up, you fool!" hissed Forden. "There will be nobody left to kill and nobody to do the killing if you don't get over there and douse those flames."

Quinn risked another peek, gasping at the wall of flames that had risen on the deck. Off to starboard, he could see the pirate ship . . . its tether dragging in the water behind it as it drifted away. Quinn grimaced, cursing himself for not tying a knot. The current had been stronger than he'd hoped.

One pirate had jumped overboard and was swimming towards the ship. Three others watched him from the rail, shouting encouragement – though their shouts died away seconds later.

Quinn lifted his head higher to see why, and swallowed hard when he saw the triangular fin slicing through the water. There was to be no escape, then.

~

"Watch, report!"

Ash left her vigil at the rail to creep back towards the wheelhouse so she could better hear Jericho's words.

"Two ships."

"Two?" shouted Zain.

"Two," Jericho confirmed. "One alight, one . . . leaving."

"Crew, report."

Ash joined the others near the wheel, which Zain indicated Cleaver should take.

"Law of the sea says that we must do what we can to assist," said Zain. "There are two ships. It is unclear what their positions are. Prepare for everything from a rescue to a fight."

They nodded, faces grim, before disappearing to unearth their favorite weapons. Ash knew that they would return with an arsenal of swords and knives, and, in Ison's case, a wicked-looking spear. She noticed that Zain's huge sword was hanging in its special place on the wheelhouse wall, among the maps he had tacked up with nails.

"You –"

"I know," Ash interrupted, shaking her head sadly. "Stay here."

"In an ideal world, we would all stay here," said Zain. "I do not wish to board either of those ships unless we have to do so. But if we do have to, I need someone on board to man the wheel."

Ash perked up. "The wheel?" she said. "You're going to put me in charge of the ship?"

"I have no choice," sighed Zain. "I will need every available sailor. So watch closely, Ash – you're about to receive a crash course in how to steer a ship. And you need to get it right."

Ash gulped. "I know how to sail a skiff," she admitted.

"Good. At least you have some knowledge of how the sails work then – what you need to keep in mind is that a skiff is fast and highly maneuverable. The *Libertas* is not. Once she sets a course, it takes much longer to change direction. Now watch this . . ."

Ash tried to concentrate as Zain set the ship through a series of movements, showing her which way to turn the wheel to achieve each one. She was aware of the crew returning, watching with disbelief as the lesson unfolded, but she tried her best to block them out.

Zain trusted her to do this and she would not let him down.

"Right," he said. "Your turn. All you need to do for now is to hold her steady."

He stood aside and looked at her expectantly. Ash could hear indignant whispers in the watching group.

"Anyone have any objections?" Zain asked, reaching for his sword. The whispers died down.

Shaking, Ash took the wheel, feeling the wood thrum under her fingers. The wheel moved sharply to starboard and she pushed it back. It was harder than she'd expected to keep it straight, and required constant pressure.

"Okay," said Zain, eyes on the ships ahead of them, now well and truly in focus. "Take her gently to port."

Ash tilted the wheel to the left and the *Libertas* slowly but surely began to veer in that direction. "The faster the ship is moving, the less pressure you need to steer," said Zain. "If we were crawling, you would need to give the wheel more swing."

Ash nodded.

"Okay," Zain said, clapping his hands for attention. "They'll have seen us by now. Straighten her up and hold her steady."

She did so and watched openmouthed as Zain ducked through the wheelhouse door, sword in hand. "Aren't you going to stay?"

"I'll be back to teach you how to stop," he said, with a devilish grin. "For now, you have the ship."

On her own, in charge of an enormous ship and all the lives aboard, Ash could do nothing but nod. Every muscle in her body tensed with effort, and she stood like a statue, eyes focused on the waves ahead. She was aware of the crew rushing about the deck, preparing for any eventuality, but could hear nothing over the roaring in her ears.

"Ah, Ash," said Cleric Greenfield, suddenly appearing in the doorway. "Zain told me you were here. I thought you might like some company."

Ash's muscles relaxed a little. Cleric Greenfield might not know one end of a ship from the other, but at least she was no longer alone with her responsibility. As the fear left her body, Ash could feel something else creeping in: pride that Zain had trusted her with the *Libertas* . . . and, she had to admit, a tiny bit of excitement.

~

"Sail! Sail! Sail!"

The Gelynion sailor was screaming from the bow, jumping up and down.

Quinn sat up. From his lofty wheelhouse roof seat, he could see the sailor was right.

It had worked! The *Libertas* was bearing down on the *Black Hawk* at speed – heading back to them.

Mind spinning, Quinn watched as Forden's crew ran to the port side, which was now facing the oncoming ship, hanging over the rail, shouting at the tops of their lungs to the *Libertas*, as it drew ever nearer. The pirates, busy throwing buckets of water over the last of the flames on the sodden deck, soon joined them.

Forden and Morpeth stood together, surveying the smoldering remains of a mast, and the surface damage to the ship's deck, deep in conversation.

Heart racing, Quinn stood and began silently waving his hands above his head. He daren't risk jumping, lest his thumping up and down attracted the attention of Dinoh, who had returned to his place at the wheel, under Quinn's feet, as soon as the fire had been brought under control.

Quinn had been surprised at the way in which the two crews had worked together to put it out — and so quickly. When he'd come up with his plan, he hadn't factored in the dampness of the masts and deck, slick with sea spray and blood. After that initial burst of heat and sparks, the fire had slowed. Once the pirates had realized that escape was not an option for them either, they had all turned their efforts to containing the fire.

Quinn had been both relieved — and horrified. He knew that as soon as calm was restored, thoughts would turn to how the fire had started. So far he'd been completely forgotten in the chaos of the pirate attack, and then the fire. But for how long?

Keeping one wary eye on Morpeth and Forden, who now seemed to be arguing, he continued to wave his arms overhead.

His one hope was that the *Libertas* saw him before Forden did.

~

"Watch, report!"

Zain's order boomed across the *Libertas*, and Ash craned forward to hear Jericho's response. She had relaxed into her duty, and was even beginning to enjoy the feel of being in charge of the powerful ship. Cleric Greenfield had helped with that, she admitted, distracting her fears with chatter of this and that, even as the *Libertas* crew prepared for battle.

"Smoke all but gone," said Jericho. "First ship drifting to present port side. Second ship drifting away to starboard. Welcoming committee. And . . . lots of birds."

Ash noted that Zain did not ask the usual question about the flag of origin on the destination ship. And she knew why. The *Black Hawk* had been recognizable across the water from leagues away. She'd known it as soon as she'd seen it – mostly because she'd never forget it. Her first sight of the Gelynion ship had been in the frozen north, when it had looked like a ghost ship sailing on land! Closer inspection had revealed a canal, cut from the harbor to behind Kurt's village, but she still felt the *Black Hawk* had a spooky, menacing air about it. Perhaps some magic as well . . . The Verdanians were still unsure as to how Forden had sailed into Barbarin and spirited Quinn away without being seen.

Now, though, it was squarely in sights, having turned sideways with the current. In fact . . . "Er, Zain," she called out. "It might be time for that lesson in stopping now."

"Wait!" Jericho called out suddenly from the watch. "There's a figure. On the wheelhouse. Away from the others."

Zain rushed to the rail, spyglass at his eye.

"Ah," he said lowering it, and turning to face the waiting crew with a satisfied smile. "Quinn Freeman."

Ash's legs felt weak, while Cleric Greenfield clapped his hands.

"I knew we would find him," said the cleric. "There was never any doubt."

Not for you, perhaps, thought Ash. "No, of course not," she said out loud.

"Tomas!" Zain was saying. "Do you recognize that other ship?"

Tomas left his station where he was helping the crew line up weapons, to look through the spyglass.

"Pirates," he said.

"You know them?" Zain asked.

"*Of* them," Tomas said. "Those men have no honor – they even steal from other pirates. They have so much gold, their captain has even painted his teeth with it. They call him the Golden Serpent."

Ash tried to imagine what that would look like.

"Er, Ash," said Cleric Greenfield, breaking into her thoughts. "I think we might need to get Zain in here before we plow into that other boat."

Ash's eyes widened as she realized just how close the *Black Hawk* was to their prow.

It was already too late to call Zain.

~

Quinn's arms dropped to his side as he watched the *Libertas* plunge relentlessly forward. Surely they should be slowing down by now? Was Zain's plan to ram the *Black Hawk*? Did he think Quinn was already dead?

He began jumping up and down, frantically, heedless of the noise he was making. "Stop! Stop!" he screamed. "I'm here! I'm alive!"

Down below, along the rail, twenty sailors were also imploring the *Libertas* to stop.

And still the boat sailed on.

Dinoh stuck his head out of the wheelhouse, looking up to see what was making the noise on his roof – and met Quinn's eyes. Startled, Dinoh took a step back, stumbling over a length of rope that had been left underfoot. He landed with an *oooof!* and opened his mouth to scream for Forden. No sound came out. Clutching his stomach, he tried again, but Quinn recognized the symptoms of being winded from one particularly trying training session on the *Libertas*. Ajax had picked him up and thrown him over his shoulder, ostensibly giving Quinn a chance to learn how to land on his feet. Only Quinn hadn't, landing on his back hard enough to knock all the breath from his body.

It had only taken one experience like that to drive home to Quinn the importance of practicing such a skill. Which was why he could now somersault – or "perform acrobatics" as Zain would have it – with ease.

Dinoh had no such skills – which bought Quinn a few more minutes. He prayed it would be long enough.

⁓

Ash tried to stay calm, eyes on the rapidly looming *Black Hawk*. Zain was at the stern of the *Libertas*, rallying the crew. She needed to do something now.

She tried to think. When sailing the skiff, all she'd had to do to slow down was to pull in the sails – but there would be no time to take in the *Libertas*'s three huge sails. She needed to try something different.

She heard a shout outside. The crew had gathered at the bow, and quickly appraised the situation. Running feet told her that help was coming. But would it come soon enough?

"Might be time to stop." Cleric Greenfield's voice, behind her, was calm.

"I don't know how!"

"Just stay calm. It will come to you."

She'd already tried that! She tilted the wheel slightly to starboard, amazed at the quick response of the ship.

And that's when she decided what to do.

Ash pulled the wheel to the right, praying the *Libertas* would turn in time. It wheeled to starboard. Turning to look behind her, she could see the ship's wide wake skew across itself, almost at right angles.

The wind immediately dropped from the sails as the ship's momentum took her sideways, thrusting towards the *Black Hawk*. Ash held her breath. If the *Libertas* didn't slow in time, she would ram side-on into the *Black Hawk*, reducing both ships to splinters.

"Interesting maneuver," said Zain, breathlessly, arriving at the wheelhouse.

"I call it the 'emergency stop,'" Ash managed, holding on to the wheel for dear life.

"Let's hope it works," he said, nudging her aside and taking her place at the wheel.

"It works on a skiff," she said, watching as a great wall of water rose up before the side of the *Libertas* that faced the disabled ship. "That water wall will stop us."

"Yes," agreed Zain. "Hopefully, it will also put out any remaining fire without drowning everyone on board the *Black Hawk*. Now get down to the rail and keep an eye on Quinn."

Dashing to the rail, Ash tried desperately to see through the water. She was dripping wet in seconds, salt water running into her eyes and down her neck. The *Libertas* barreled forward, plowing a bubbling, foaming furrow through the ocean. Blinking rapidly, Ash focused her gaze on the wheelhouse roof – and saw a slight figure jumping up and down, waving with one arm while he seemed to be holding up his breeches with the other.

It was unmistakably Quinn.

Ash leapt up and down, screaming and waving, wanting to let Quinn know that she'd seen him.

"He can't hear you," came a sly voice at her elbow. "And that big Gelynion will kill him anyway."

Ash wheeled around to face Kurt, standing beside her, pinched face alight with malice.

"We're going to save him," she said, fiercely. "You just watch."

He shrugged and sauntered away, disappearing below deck. Dismissing him from her thoughts, she turned her attention back to Quinn – and saw that Kurt's prophecy was about to come true. A large, gray-haired Gelynion sailor was climbing up onto the wheelhouse roof, a knife between his teeth!

"Oh, Quinn," she whispered, watching as her friend sidled to the far side of his platform, watching the Gelynion. More Gelynions, and Morpeth, the huge Deslonder, were racing across the deck towards the pair, weapons in hand.

Quinn was cornered, and there was nothing she could do to help him!

Chapter Twelve

Quinn was struggling to breathe, fear closing his throat. Crouched low, he kept both eyes on Dinoh as the Gelynion hauled himself up onto the wheelhouse roof, cursing at Quinn through the teeth clenched around his knife. One more huge effort and he'd be level with Quinn and that gleaming knife would be coming his way.

Quinn knew he needed to act – and fast! – but it was as though time had slowed down, rendering him incapable of moving. He could hear a wild roar in his ears and knew that the huge wave kicked up by the *Libertas* when Zain had pulled that weird sideways maneuver was nearly upon them. Down below, pounding feet and shouting told him that Dinoh had not been alone in spotting him up here – and reinforcements were on the way.

He was trapped.

He tried to breathe, tried to think, but it was as though his brain had shriveled to nothing. Above the roar of the wave, he thought he could hear someone shrieking his name, but perhaps it was just one of the seabirds – when he'd let them go, they'd been so confused by the smoke that they'd simply been circling the sky above the ship.

He heard a deep grunt as Dinoh pulled himself up another few inches, weight on his forearms.

Now, thought Quinn, and his body moved as though of its own volition. Hands held up defensively, he stepped once, twice, across the roof, and then brought his right leg up, kicking out with all that he had. He felt his boot connect with Dinoh's jaw, heard the crack as the man's head flew backward and watched in amazement as the Gelynion flew through the air to land in a heap on the deck.

Quinn withdrew to the center of the roof, heart pumping. He felt energized, ready for anything, amazed at his own ability to take down a man twice his size. He spun slowly around, dancing on the balls of his feet, looking to see where the next attack was coming from – just as Zain had taught him.

All the things he'd learned in training had become instinct, just as Zain had told him they would. Quinn felt unstoppable.

And then he heard Zain's voice in his mind, as though the captain was standing next to him. "Overconfidence often leads to embarrassment at best – and a bloody, painful death at worst."

Quinn took a slow, calming breath as the first of the Gelynions reached the wheelhouse. Then a second. And a third. Looking out, Quinn realized that every man standing, including Forden, Morpeth and the pirate with the gold teeth was headed his way.

He was not going to be able to fight his way out of this one.

Desperately, he looked around, searching for an escape. The roar in his ears became louder, and he realized that he had been so focused on the fight that he'd forgotten about the wall of water coming their way.

He turned quickly – and just managed a quick gulp of air before he was knocked off his feet as water engulfed the *Black Hawk*. Tumbled over and over, eyes closed against the burning pain of the salt, Quinn had no idea which way was up. Pain shot through his side as he connected with something solid – the remains of the mast? He tried desperately to grab hold of it but it was torn from his grasp as the water pushed forward. Something grabbed at his ankle, and he drew his feet up to his chest to evade the groping hand.

Chest burning, Quinn tried to blow bubbles – anything to tell him which way was up – but he couldn't see in the froth around him. He felt as though his brain was going to explode out of his ears, so great was the pressure. Once again, his body slammed into something hard and this time he managed to hook one arm around it, clinging on for dear life. It was smooth to touch, and he realized he'd gotten hold of the ship's rail – the starboard rail.

Thanking whichever lucky star had saved him from being washed overboard, Quinn cautiously opened his eyes, noticing as he did so that the wave was receding. All around him, dazed Gelynions and pirates were struggling to their feet. He spotted Yergon, crouched low, clinging to a mast, and the little man nodded at him.

Quinn knew he'd need to act fast if he was going to get off this ship. The *Libertas* was floating off the port side of the *Black Hawk*, and he could see Zain and the crew preparing to board.

He remembered the *Black Hawk* deck as it had been minutes before, slick with blood, littered with bodies and smoldering ash. He didn't want his friends to end up like that and, despite their losses, the Gelynions and the pirates still outnumbered the Verdanians more than three to one.

No, he wasn't going to let Zain and the others fight a battle because of him. He would get off the *Black Hawk* himself.

The question was how.

A screech from overhead drew his attention and he noticed the birds were still wheeling around the remaining masts as though nothing had happened. And that's when he saw it – one of the pirate's grappling ropes was hanging high in the *Black Hawk*'s fourth mast, the smaller one in the stern.

Scrambling to his feet, he ran as fast as he could towards that mast. A Gelynion sailor lunged at his legs as he bolted past, but Quinn saw a quick movement from the corner of his eye and the sailor fell flat on his face. Yergon retracted his foot, which he'd used to trip the sailor, and nodded once again at Quinn, who took heart from the support and darted forward, slipping a little on the sodden deck as he ran, looking neither left nor right, eyes on the mast.

He was nearly there, just another ten or so paces, then nine, then eight, then seven, then . . .

Morpeth loomed up in front of him like a bad dream, carrying what looked like an oar from the longboat over his shoulder.

"Going somewhere, Monstruo Mouse?" he asked in Suspite.

Quinn couldn't speak. He had to get around Morpeth to get up that mast, and he had to do it fast.

He feinted to the right – Morpeth removed the oar from over his shoulder, and swung it at him. Quinn ducked and felt the breeze from the oar tickle the back of his neck as it passed over him.

"Ah, Monstruo Mouse has some moves, does he?" chortled Morpeth. "Well, let us see how well you dance, little mouse." He swung the oar hard and low, sweeping it at Quinn's legs.

Quinn jumped, but the oar struck his left leg, a glancing blow that brought tears to his eyes.

"Ha!" said Morpeth, "Try this!" Morpeth stepped forward, thrusting the oar at Quinn's stomach. Morpeth came at him again and again, forcing him backward across the deck. In desperation, Quinn grabbed the end of the oar, shouting in pain as the thin edges cut his palms, pushing the oar hard to one side.

Thrown off balance, Morpeth stumbled sideways and fell to the deck and Quinn took his advantage, darting in behind the big man, grabbing the bottom of the grappling hook rope and clambering up the mast, his hands slick with blood, rope between his teeth. Each movement was agony but he had no time to think about it, knowing he had to get out of Morpeth's reach.

Below, he heard the huge Deslonder's rage-filled roar, but he tried to put it out of his mind, concentrating on putting one painful hand on top of the other, thrusting upward with his legs, thanking Ash for all the times she'd made him race her to the top of the *Libertas*'s main mast.

The mast began shaking and he knew that he was being followed. Gritting his teeth, he climbed the final few paces to the second crossbar, where he'd seen the grappling hook. Resting a moment to draw the rope up with him in a loop, he slung it over his shoulder. Then, one hand on the mast, he stood on the crossbar and tried to tug the grappling hook towards him. Once, twice, three times he pulled, but he couldn't loosen its grip on the sail.

Quinn wanted to curse, but no words were strong enough at that point. He was going to have to climb out there to unhook it and then throw it as hard as he could at the *Libertas*, hoping to reach a mast on his ship. Below, he could see the *Libertas* crew, half of them watching him openmouthed, the others racing to trim the sails, trying to keep the ship as steady as possible.

He noticed that Zain had lined the ships up, pulling in as close as he could to the *Black Hawk* without the pirates and Gelynions below being able to board. Abel was running up and down the rail, throwing off grappling hooks and tethering lines, ensuring the *Libertas* was safe. One quick glance down the mast was enough to see that it was the gold-toothed pirate captain who was following him up to his perch. He was close enough for Quinn to see the amber color of the one eye that was not covered by a patch.

The mast continued to shake and sway as Quinn got down on his stomach and began crawling along the crossbar towards the hook. He could hear nothing over the roar of blood in his ears, see nothing except the hook, feel nothing but the thin bar under him. The *Black Hawk* continued to rock up and down on the waves, the birds continued to circle overhead, but Quinn concentrated on his breathing. Slow and steady.

For the second time that day, time stopped. There was just Quinn and the grappling hook, Quinn and his mind, Quinn and his breath.

And then he was there, the hook in his hand, and suddenly he could hear the pirate cursing at him as he climbed the mast, just below Quinn's crossbar. Glancing down, Quinn saw that the man had removed his eye patch, and was now watching him unswervingly with two beady eyes – one amber, one as dark as coal. Quinn shivered, feeling the evil in that black eye.

There was no time to waste. Quinn took the rope from his shoulder, keeping it looped in his hand, and then gingerly stood, thanking Zain for all those hours he'd spent practicing balancing. As the pirate reached the crutch of the crossbar behind him, he swung the grappling hook three times, swaying with each movement, and then let the hook fly.

Behind him, the pirate cursed again as he realized that if he wanted Quinn, he was going to have to follow him out there. Down on his hands and knees, the pirate began crawling along the crossbar, his extra weight making it sway.

Quinn ignored him, eyes glued to the hook, which seemed to fly like a bird to the *Libertas* – where it lodged in the sail, tearing a jagged stripe down its face.

Quinn's heart sank. The sail wouldn't hold his weight. He saw Dilly run for the mast, scurrying up it as fast as he could. If he could get there fast enough, then maybe he'd be able to secure the hook for Quinn to . . .

A hand reached for his ankle.

Quinn felt the brush of fingers on the back of his boot, and slid his foot farther forward, his eyes on Dilly, who was climbing towards the grappling hook.

There was no time to lose.

Grasping the rope in both his painful hands, Quinn wrapped his legs around it, and jumped.

~

Ash thought she was going to be sick all over the deck.

She couldn't watch. She *had* to watch. Zain had put her back in charge of the wheel, and she was holding the ship as steady as she could.

All around her men were shouting up at Dilly, who was climbing the mast faster than he'd ever climbed before. But Quinn had jumped and his weight on the rope was tearing the sail, dragging the grappling hook down, down, down towards the deck.

He couldn't make it. The lower the hook slid, the more chance Quinn had of being dashed against the side of the *Libertas*.

Behind him, pirates and Gelynions were screaming, trying to reach for him as he swung just above their heads and out over the water that now seemed to stretch like a gulf between the two ships. The hook slid again.

One hand over her mouth, one on the wheel, Ash shifted her glance to Dilly, who was now in line with the hook and reaching out desperately from the mast, trying to grab it to secure it to something solid.

And still Quinn fell.

Dilly crawled along the crossbeam, just as Quinn had done, and grabbed hold of the hook with one hand. But it simply pulled him forward, and he nearly fell from his own precarious perch.

On the *Black Hawk*, the pirates and Gelynions had begun throwing missiles at Quinn, using anything they could get their hands on. A gleaming knife cut through the air, sailing past Quinn's head with just a hand span to spare. He didn't seem to notice, focused instead on the water – which was getting closer and closer.

Suddenly, he jerked upward on the rope with a snap.

Ash's eyes flew to the mast – to find that Dilly had jumped! He'd gone backward off the crossbeam, clinging to the hook, providing a counterweight to Quinn's downward spiral.

⁓

Quinn tried desperately to hitch himself farther up the rope as it snapped upward, bringing him directly in line with the *Libertas*'s rail. He could hear the panicked shouts, could feel the wind pushing his hair straight back, could see in his mind his body thudding into the rail, breaking into tiny pieces. He had to get higher!

Quinn flicked his legs up, trying to bring his body up above the rail – not enough. He swung them back and flicked again, this time with as much force as he could muster, and felt his feet go up, up, up – and over, as he backflipped up over the rail with such force that he did a complete somersault, landing in a sodden, shaking heap at the feet of the waiting crew, still clutching the end of the rope as though his life depended on it.

There was a strange silence as everyone stared down at him, seemingly stunned that he was there, before Zain stepped forward to gently take the rope from his hands, handing it to Abel, who climbed the mast high enough to lower Dilly gently to the deck.

"So, Quinn Freeman, you return," said Zain, and Quinn could hear the relief in his voice. "And with jester's acrobatics."

Quinn lifted his head, managing a tired smile for his captain. "Youthful exuberance," he said, echoing Cleric Greenfield's words. "And it came in handy."

Zain roared with laughter as the crew moved in to surround Quinn. Jericho was slapping him on the back, Cleaver ruffling his hair. Dilly and Abel joined the group, and Quinn held out a bloody hand almost shyly to Dilly, who grasped it firmly. Quinn knew that it was Dilly's climbing ability and quick thinking that had saved him today.

"But where's Ash?" asked Quinn. "Where is he?"

There was a pause. "Er, *she* is holding the wheel," said Zain.

Quinn frowned, then realized that nobody else had batted an eyelid at the *she*. It seemed as though Ash's secret was out.

"Which reminds me," Zain continued. "We'd best get ourselves out of here."

As one, they suddenly became aware of the threat from the other boat, sailors of all kinds still hanging over the sides, shouting and throwing things. Ash had managed to keep the *Libertas* steady, but the drift of the ocean was drawing the two ships closer together, making an invasion imminent.

Zain raced to the wheelhouse, with Cleaver on his heels, shouting directions at the crew, who leapt into action to get the *Libertas* underway. Quinn sat where he was, feeling dazed, until Ash, relieved from her duties, dropped beside him and threw her arms around him.

"I guess a hug's okay now they know you're a girl," he said, trying for lightness, despite his weariness, "but you don't have to squeeze me to death."

She slapped him lightly on the arm. "I don't plan to make a habit of it," she said. "I'm just happy to see you!"

"And I'm happy to be here," he said, seriously, flopping onto his back. "I didn't really think I'd ever see any of you again."

"Oh, Quinn, were you scared?"

Quinn opened his mouth to speak, and then paused. "Worse than that," he admitted slowly. "I felt . . . hopeless. Without hope. It's the worst feeling in the world." There was a small silence, as he disappeared into his memories.

"Well, you're back with us now," Ash said, dragging him back. "We started looking straightaway, you know. I – that is, we – never gave up hope."

Quinn smiled at her, sitting up to pat her on the shoulder. "I guess that's the secret then," he said. "As long as someone has hope for you, there's a chance things will turn out okay."

As he removed his hand, he realized he'd left a bloody print on her shirt.

"Sorry," he muttered.

"You're hurt!" she said. "We need to get you cleaned up – and what exactly happened to your breeches? And your boots!"

"In a minute," he said, standing up and hobbling over to the rail. "I just want to watch as we leave the *Black Hawk* far behind us."

They stood together at the rail, each deep in thought, and watched the crippled ship grow smaller and smaller.

"Do you think they'll be all right?" Ash asked.

Quinn turned to her, feeling bitter and angry and confused. "I don't really care," he said, before turning his back to the rail and walking away. Even as he said the words, his mind conjured up an image of Yergon, nodding at him, offering both wordless support and help to get away. He did hope the little man was all right. Surely he would be, now that Forden needed a mapmaker again?

"Come on," he said to Ash, who was looking worried. "I need a wash. And a clean pair of socks." *And to think about something else*, he added silently.

Ash laughed, and led the way down to his cabin. As Quinn followed, he noticed Kurt watching them from the shadows of the wheelhouse. He suppressed the urge to walk over and punch the Northern boy, knowing that he would soon have his chance to talk to Zain.

And, if Quinn's eyes didn't deceive him, the Northern boy looked worried.

Chapter Thirteen

"He stole my map!" said Quinn, pointing at Kurt, who was staring at him defiantly from the other side of Zain's cabin.

"Did not," Kurt responded in Suspite. "It's right there."

He pointed to the smudged, bedraggled parchment lying on Zain's desk. Quinn rolled his eyes.

"This is your map, is it not?" asked Zain, mildly.

"Yes, but . . . He must have copied it!"

"Copied it?"

"Copied it," confirmed Quinn. "And gave it to Odilon."

"Odilon?" Now Zain was looking confused.

"Yes," said Quinn. "Who gave it to the Gelynions."

Zain leaned back in his chair. "Why would Odilon do that?"

"To get you out of the race," said Quinn. "At least, I think that's why. They just kept saying 'no mapmaker, no map.' And then he took Ajax."

"Odilon took Ajax?"

"Yes," said Quinn, impatiently. "I already told you all this. Ira pushed me in the pit and escaped. Odilon took Ajax."

"Ah, so much for the alliance," said Zain, who didn't look as concerned at this information as Quinn thought he should.

"Yes, your approach to keep them close didn't work," said Quinn. "It just gave them a chance to betray you."

"And to hurt you," agreed Zain. "For that I am truly sorry."

Quinn dropped his gaze. "Nobody could have known they'd do that," he said. "Except him!" He pointed at Kurt again.

"So you say," said Kurt, staring at him impassively.

Quinn could see that there was no way that Kurt would admit his guilt. And no way, without the copied map, that Quinn could prove it – and given that he'd used the map to set fire to the *Black Hawk*, that wasn't going to happen.

Zain looked back and forth between the two of them. He paused. "Kurt, you will remove your things from Quinn's cabin and move down to crew's quarters."

Quinn sighed with relief. He'd been horrified to arrive in his cabin to find Tomas sheepishly making his bed and Kurt's fingerprints all over his map. Ash had pulled him away, taking him down to Cleric Greenfield's cabin to dress his wounds, but he was still hurt and angry at the invasion of his space. Ash had wanted him to rest, but he had insisted on going to see Zain straightaway.

Now, Kurt opened his mouth to speak, but Zain held up a finger. "I know, there is no proof of Quinn's accusations, but the two of you cannot share a cabin with this open animosity between you – and the cabin belongs to the mapmaker, and the mapmaker is Quinn."

He looked over at Quinn's hands, wrapped in strips of clean fabric and soothed with some kind of healing salve that Ash had cooked up. "Or will be," Zain went on smoothly. "As soon as he can hold a quill."

Quinn was itching to get back to his map – his real map, the one hidden away in Cleric Greenfield's cabin – to record his memories, but for now he was stuck with planning. He just wanted things to be normal again. Or as normal as they could be when they were still who knew how far away from Markham.

Kurt said nothing, but his stare was hostile. Quinn raised his chin, meeting Kurt's flat gaze with a challenge of his own. He would not forget the trials he had suffered because of this boy's actions. His head still hurt, his hands still hurt, his legs had bite marks all over them. He'd spent weeks in the dark, at the hands of strangers, and, frankly, he wanted someone to pay.

He was only sorry that he did not have the proof he needed to convince Zain that Kurt was a liar and a threat to all aboard the *Libertas*.

But Quinn would be watching him closely from now on. And he wanted Kurt to know it.

"Leave us," said Zain, cutting through the silence, nodding at Kurt, who scowled and slunk from the cabin.

"He's lying," said Quinn, as soon as the door shut behind Kurt. "You know he is. How can you believe him?"

"What I *know* is that he is still in possession of the map," said Zain. "What I *believe* is – unless you can suddenly read minds – known only to myself."

Quinn said nothing, consumed with anger and disappointment. Part of him wanted to tell Zain about the real map, but he couldn't be sure that Kurt wasn't lurking outside the door, listening in. Events of the past few weeks had taught him that the fewer people who knew about that map, the better. He would tell Zain at a time when he could be sure they were completely alone.

"You are angry," Zain continued. "And I understand that feeling very well. But do not direct your anger at Kurt."

"Why not?" Quinn shot back. "It was all his fault."

"As you say," said Zain. "But you are back now, in one piece – albeit a thinner piece than you were – and we are all more than pleased to see you. But we need to concentrate on what matters now, and that's completing our journey. Time is ticking away on our one year . . ." Zain picked up the quill on his desk, running the feather through his fingers while he seemed to search for words. "Quinn," he began, before placing the quill precisely in front of him. "We need to talk about that fire."

Quinn had been waiting for this. It was one of the reasons he'd wanted this conversation over. He said nothing.

"You set it to raise a signal for us," said Zain, slowly. "Didn't you?"

I did, Quinn thought. But remembering the overwhelming feeling of despair and desperation that had driven him to light the fire, he could not respond.

"Because, while it was a brave move, it also carried a stupidly high degree of risk," Zain went on. "But you know that."

Quinn nodded briefly. "I . . . had no choice," he prevaricated. "There was no escape."

Zain's eyes probed his, seeming to want to see into Quinn's mind. "And yet, here you are. All escaped."

Quinn shifted uncomfortably, and Zain nodded. "We will speak no more of it," he said. "But remember this: the only man who is truly trapped is the man who does nothing. If you do *something* – anything – then you force change."

Quinn tried to concentrate. He was suddenly overwhelmingly tired, as though the burst of energy that had brought him safely back to the *Libertas* had been his last. He slumped back against the wall as Zain's voice washed over him.

"Quinn? Are you okay?"

Dizzy and nauseous, Quinn shook his head, causing a sharp pain above his ear.

Zain cursed under his breath. "You need rest," he said. "I told you that we should do this later."

He had, Quinn acknowledged as his legs began to give way beneath him, but Quinn hadn't wanted to wait; his fury at Kurt had driven him onward.

Almost in tears now, he wondered if this stormy maelstrom of feelings would ever go away. He thought back to how he'd been before he'd set foot on the *Libertas* – uncertain, afraid, a little bit shy, happy with his life in Markham. Now he knew that he could do more than he'd ever imagined possible – but he would have given anything to go back to being *that* Quinn, rather than the Quinn he was right now.

"Come," said Zain, his voice almost gentle. "It is time to sleep, Quinn Freeman. Everything will look clearer in the morning."

⁓

Quinn flexed his fingers, wriggling them tentatively. Satisfied, he picked up his quill, dipping it carefully into the deep, vibrant blue ink that Ash had made for him. Gently stroking it across the parchment, his breath caught as the glorious color seeped and spread.

Humming to himself, he sat back in his chair – technically, Cleric Greenfield's chair – and surveyed his work. The cleric had gone up on deck, ostensibly to get some fresh air but, Quinn knew, mostly to give him time and space. He had told the cleric a little of what had gone on during his time on the *Black Hawk*, and had also told him everything he'd learned about Odilon's role in Quinn's kidnapping – and Kurt's.

As always, Cleric Greenfield had vowed to write a letter to the King. Quinn had smiled. The cleric had written several letters to the King during their time away from home. All, of course, remained unsent. But nobody had the heart to tell the little man he was wasting his time.

Quinn shook his head at the thought, and returned to his map. He was proud of this map, his *real* map. Full of detail and awash with lush color, it was the very best work he could do. He'd taken great care to put in small illustrations of relevant details – a tiny picture of Nammu rising from the deep, the triangle-shaped structures from the first village they'd discovered, the icy domes of Kurt's frozen home.

Ajax would have done better with the drawings, Quinn acknowledged, but he was happy nonetheless as he drew a smiling serpent on Tomas's homeland, taking pleasure in writing "Barbarin" in careful letters beside it.

A tiny, illustrated pirate ship now sailed forevermore just beyond the place where two oceans, in different shades of blue and green, rushed towards each other.

Quinn had been back on the *Libertas* for five days now, and he was pleased at how well his hands were healing. He'd slept solidly for most of the first two days, and then eaten solidly for the next two. To his surprise, Cook had been encouraging him to visit as often as he liked.

"It's because he's got *me* to avoid now instead of you," Ash had said morosely when he'd mentioned it.

Quinn had noticed that half the crew now went out of their way not to be near Ash. "He'll get over it," he'd said to her. "They all will."

She shook her head. "I don't think they will. It's too ingrained. They think girls are bad luck on ships."

"Yes, well, they thought I was full of magic, but they seem to have managed to forget that," he said. "Just give it time."

It was true that Dilly and Cook had welcomed Quinn back into the fold. He had sought Dilly out a few days ago, to thank him properly for his part in Quinn's escape. The sailor had merely nodded.

"You might be a freak," he said, a small smile softening his words, "but I saw you up there and remembered that you are *our* freak."

"Thanks," said Quinn, flinching. "I think."

Dilly had roared with laughter, slapped him on the back and walked away.

Later that day, Quinn had been sitting alone outside the galley, trying to fill his endless hunger with gruel. Zain had warned him that the ship was on short rations, and had been very interested in Quinn's revelation that the *Black Hawk* had also been a very hungry ship.

"Here," Cook had said, emerging from his kingdom behind the galley door, and slopping a second helping into Quinn's bowl.

"Thanks," said Quinn, gulping it down.

Cook had sat down on the deck beside him. "I have not been fair to you," he said, slowly.

"Oh, that's –" Quinn began.

"Let me finish," said Cook, holding up his spoon. "Do you know my real name?"

Quinn thought a moment. "No," he admitted.

"It's Cook. Just Cook. Just as my mother was before me."

Quinn nodded.

"When she was alive, I was Cook's Boy. Just Cook's Boy. If I ever had a name, it was lost early on."

Cook stared across the deck, out to the endless horizon. "My mother believed in magic," he went on. "She was stuck in a workhouse, cooking slop for people who were being worked to death, and she still believed in magic and witchcraft. It killed her in the end. She took some potion made for her by a supposed witch and she died. And that's when I became Cook. And I've distrusted the idea of magic ever since."

Quinn said nothing.

"But you are not magic," said Cook. "I watched you cling to the end of that rope and I realized that you are just a boy. A boy who can think fast."

With that, Cook had lumbered to his feet and gone back to the galley, leaving Quinn to contemplate his cooling gruel – and the idea of life without a real name.

Now, Quinn put the finishing touches to his island, and thought about another conversation with Cook – about melting gold. After a little persuading, Zain had given Quinn a small quantity of the gold dust that Frey had sent with Tomas, and he was planning to illuminate his map with touches of gold.

Cook was keen to help "cook" the gold, but Quinn had told him and Zain that he'd paint the gold on "at the end," knowing he'd otherwise have to waste some on his fake map.

Just thinking about how beautiful his map would be made Quinn smile, as he carefully inserted the cork back into the ink pot, wincing a little as the movement set off a wave of pain in his head. He knew Ash was more worried about the bump he'd received falling from the mast than about any other injury he'd suffered.

"Damage to the head can be strange," she said. "One minute you're fine, the next . . . well, things aren't working like they used to."

He pushed her words from his mind once again, trying to forget the dizziness and bright flashes of light he kept seeing. He hadn't told her about them – well, not all the details. He didn't want her to worry and, frankly, he didn't really want to think about it. The one thing he'd always been able to rely upon was his memory.

Quinn shook his head, wincing at the starbursts of pain. He'd had no problem updating his map: the pictures in his mind were as clear as ever.

It would be fine. He'd be fine, now that he was back where he belonged.

He would go back upstairs and make some similar changes to the map in his cabin, Quinn decided. He'd done his best to smooth Kurt's fingerprints from the fake map, but he was going to have to live with the lines the Northern boy had drawn to approximate the coastline they'd left behind.

It didn't matter, he supposed, that map wasn't meant to be accurate anyway.

Quinn was finding it easier than he'd imagined to avoid Kurt. But that didn't mean he'd forgiven the Northern boy. Patience, that's what he needed. That's what his da would tell him.

Quinn smiled, thinking of his da. Beyard Freeman was a devoted father and husband, and the hardest worker that Quinn knew. He expected nothing but the best from his sons, and each tried his hardest to give it to him. And farming had taught him patience.

Quinn could wait.

He stood, automatically patting his pocket to feel the tooth, back where it belonged, and opened the door, making his way along the passage. Even now, he reveled in his ability to move about the ship at will, opening any door he chose to open (apart from Zain's cabin). His small taste of captivity had given him a new appreciation of freedom. No wonder Zain was willing to risk everything to gain it, even if his life at the palace didn't look so bad from the outside.

Quinn veered towards the stairs to the deck. He would go and sit in the sun for a few minutes before continuing his work. He wanted to see how Abel and Ison were getting on with their new project.

Up on deck, Quinn could hear the screaming of the seabirds as they flew around Jericho in the watch. At the foot of the mast, Abel and Ison were setting up a large cage with a sliding door. When Quinn had told the *Libertas* crew about how the *Black Hawk* used seabirds to find land, Abel and Ison had vowed they would catch some so the Verdanians could do the same.

Fortunately for them, given that land was nowhere in sight, the seabirds from the *Black Hawk* were still flying aimlessly overhead, occasionally landing on the *Libertas* deck for a rest. Zain had given them permission to take apart an old wooden sea chest and they'd used the wood to construct their cage, tying it together with the wool they'd unraveled from a pair of socks that were more holes than sock.

So far, they hadn't managed to catch a single bird, but each night they reported importantly that they were "getting closer." From where Quinn was standing now, it looked as though tonight's report would be similar.

Quinn squinted up at the sun, which was dropping past the horizon earlier now, leaving a chill lingering in the air. The season was on the turn – and he felt a small pang, as he realized that he didn't even know what season they might be up to. Were the seasons the same in this part of the world? The stars weren't. He made a note to ask Tomas.

He was much happier with his new cabinmate than he had been with Kurt. Tomas was easygoing and cheerful, which surprised Quinn, given their last exchange on the path with the serpent. Then again, he thought, nobody was at their best under pressure.

He was grateful for Tomas's consideration during those first early days back on board the *Libertas*. Tomas had crept around the cabin, being careful not to wake the sleeping Quinn, and had kept the flask of water by Quinn's bed topped up and fresh.

Since Quinn had been feeling better, the two boys had discovered a shared sense of humor and Tomas had been eager to find out everything Quinn could tell him about Verdania. He was inordinately proud of the Verdanian-style clothing his mother had sewn for him before he'd left, so that he'd blend in. Quinn hadn't had the heart

226

to tell him that his array of shirts in dizzyingly bright colors weren't exactly going to disappear in a Verdanian crowd . . .

For Quinn, Tomas was also a valuable source of information and Quinn had asked him every question he could think of about his homeland – which was a lot, with new ones every day. But Quinn filed away every answer in the back of his mind, adding it to his own knowledge of the world around them.

The one subject that Tomas would not be drawn on was his father, and Quinn respected that boundary. He could see that the other boy was still struggling with the fact that his father had sent him away. Quinn had often seen him sitting with Zain, expression mournful, as Zain tried to explain why a father would do what he thought was best for his son, even if it pained him. But Quinn remembered how he'd felt that morning when he'd heard his own father discussing with Master Blau Quinn's departure from his family. At least Quinn had the knowledge that every minute he was away meant more financial security for his family. Tomas didn't have even that small comfort. In fact, Ash had told him, Frey had *paid* Zain with rugs to take Tomas.

A sudden shout from the watch drew Quinn's attention back to the deck. Jericho was standing up, one hand on the mast, the other waving frantically at the deck for attention. Quinn froze. Surely it wasn't the *Black Hawk*?

Or the Golden Serpent's pirates? Zain had been adamant that they'd be drifting at sea for a while to come.

Then he caught Jericho's words above the cawing seabirds.

"Monster! Monster!"

Quinn's breath caught as he rushed to the rail. Sure enough, there she was, rising up and out of the deep, small black eye staring unblinkingly in their direction. With a mighty slap, Nammu fell backward, sending waves ricocheting across the ocean's surface towards them.

He felt Ash crash into the railing beside him. "It's back!" she said, breathlessly.

The great white head slowly emerged from the water as Nammu lay off the starboard bow, surveying the *Libertas*. Quinn could hear the crew shouting behind him and Tomas crept up to the rail to his left.

"Have you seen her before?" Quinn asked Tomas. Quinn always thought of the creature as "she."

"No," he answered. "But I've heard stories."

"What kind of stories?" Quinn didn't take his eyes from the huge white head.

"That there was a sea monster out here," said Tomas.

Quinn looked down, to see Tomas's hands gripping the rail, the knuckles white.

"Quinn thinks it's good luck for us," said Ash.

"I *know* she is," he said, fiercely.

"I hope you're right," said Tomas. "Because otherwise we're dead."

As though she'd heard him, Nammu suddenly spouted that strange mix of mist and smoke from the top of her head, before diving down into the depths. Seconds passed before her enormous tail appeared above the waterline.

"Look," said Quinn. "She's waving!"

"Ha!" said Tomas. "Deciding whether to bat us away like flies more like."

But the big tail continued straight down, before disappearing in a whirlpool of froth and bubble.

Standing on the rail, with his two friends beside him, the dying sun still warm on his back, his real map updated and beautiful, and Kurt banished to the crew's quarters, Quinn was startled by the warm feeling that spread through him. True, the past few months had not been smooth sailing, but he'd survived.

"If you think Nammu is bad, be grateful we haven't met Genesi yet," he said aloud.

"Genesi?" Tomas was startled. "What's Genesi?"

Quinn laughed. "The dragon at the end of the world. Waiting to snap us up when we sail off the edge."

Tomas went pale. "Where's the edge?"

"We don't know," Quinn said. "Nobody does. We're just hoping that it's not in this direction."

Ash elbowed him in the ribs. "Stop it!" she said. "You're scaring him."

Quinn laughed again. "I'm scaring me!" But deep down he wasn't scared, he realized. Not really. He knew what it was like to feel really scared now, and he knew that stories couldn't hurt you – but people could.

"It's good to be scared," said a deep voice behind him. Zain had handed the wheel to Cleaver and come down to join them on the deck. "Being scared means you're alert. When you get too comfortable . . . that's when things creep up on you."

Quinn shivered, staring out at the endless ocean. It wouldn't do to get too comfortable out here.

Not that anyone could.

"You just crept up on us," joked Ash. "And we were scared."

"Yes," said Zain. "But perhaps not scared of the right things." Quinn looked up at him, startled at hearing the captain reflecting his own thoughts. Zain bared his teeth at Quinn in what was, for Zain, a huge smile.

"But come," the captain said. "Cook has prepared dinner. A delicious bowl of gruel for everyone."

Tomas groaned. "We had gruel yesterday. And the day before that."

Zain laughed. "And we shall have it again tomorrow. Or maybe not? For tomorrow is another day, and we never know what it may bring."

As Zain and his friends wandered off, Ash and Tomas bickering lightly with each other about gruel, Quinn lingered, elbows on the rail, watching the play of light on the water. He wondered if Ajax was doing the same on the *Fair Maiden*, or perhaps his friend was now in a new land or even on his way home to Verdania. Thinking of Ajax led his thoughts to Ira, but he quickly pushed away the image of the blond boy shoving him down into that pit in Barbarin. The less thought about Ira, the better.

His deep sigh lifted the hair from his cheek, and he thought that it might be time to get Ash to give him another haircut. He'd returned her knife to her, and was, once again, without a weapon, even to trim his own hair. If he got nothing else out of this journey, he vowed he was going to get himself a knife. Allyn would be jealous . . . though Allyn would have turned sixteen by the time Quinn returned, he realized, and would have a knife of his own.

It was strange to think that, if all went to plan, he'd be seeing his family again soon. Verdania could be just over the next wave – or it could be at the other end of the world for all he knew. But with not quite five moon cycles to go in their allotted year, the *Libertas* needed to be closer to home than not if they had any chance of winning the prize.

It was a sobering thought.

"Quinn!" Ash called and he turned from the rail. She was standing by the galley with a steaming bowl in each hand. "Dinner!"

Blinking his eyes to stave off the sudden pain that had forged through his head as he'd turned, he managed a smile and walked towards her, more than ready to put aside his thoughts.

Tomorrow was another day. Surely things could only get better.

Acknowledgments

This story is a work of fiction, set in a mythical, made-up world, but the mapmaking techniques that Quinn uses are loosely based on the navigation feats of those early brave sailors and explorers who first decided that there was more to the world than what they knew – and set out to discover it. We all owe them a great deal.

In bringing the story to you, I owe so much to Sophie Hamley, and the intrepid team at Hachette Australia, particularly Suzanne O'Sullivan, Kate Stevens, Chris Kunz, Ashleigh Barton, Fiona Hazard, Justin Ractliffe, Louise Sherwin-Stark and Matt Richell, who took a chance on me, as well as cover designers Blacksheep.

Every writer needs a team, and mine is large in number and big on enthusiasm.

To my family, Bev, Dennis, Bronwyn, Christine and Michael, thanks for being the world's greatest cheerleaders.

To my support crew (in alphabetical order) – Alex Brooks, Mark Dapin, Kelly Exeter, Lisa Heidke, Valerie Khoo, Allison Rushby, Kerri Sackville and Anna Spargo-Ryan – thanks for talking me down from the ceiling when required.

Thank you again to my "Pink Fibro" community, and all my friends, who have taken Quinn, Zain and the rest of the Mapmaker crew to heart. And thank you to the thousands of readers who keep asking me that most valuable of questions: "What happens next?"

And, as always, thanks and love, to my boys: John, Joseph and Lucas. I'm glad you're with me on this wild ride.

Collect the Whole Series

A. L. Tait, who writes fiction and nonfiction for adults under another name, grew up dreaming of world domination. Unfortunately, at the time there were only alphabet sisters B. L. and C. A. and long-suffering brother M. D. M. to practice on . . . and parents who didn't look kindly upon sword fights, plank walking or thumbscrews. But dreams don't die and The Mapmaker Chronicles, the author's first series of books for children, is the result.

A. L. Tait lives in country NSW, Australia, with a family, a garden and four goldfish.